Aurora

ISBN: 978-1-7781566-5-6

Orbis Tertius Press

AURORA

Ryan Madej

Orbis Tertius Press

Alberta, Canada

"*This is why a tainted society has invented psychiatry to defend itself against the investigations of certain superior intellects whose faculties of divination would be troublesome.*"

- Antonin Artaud

"*In the perfect couple, what disappears in the one appears in the other.*"

- Jean Baudrillard

PART ONE

THE BALLROOMS OF MARS (1995-2000)

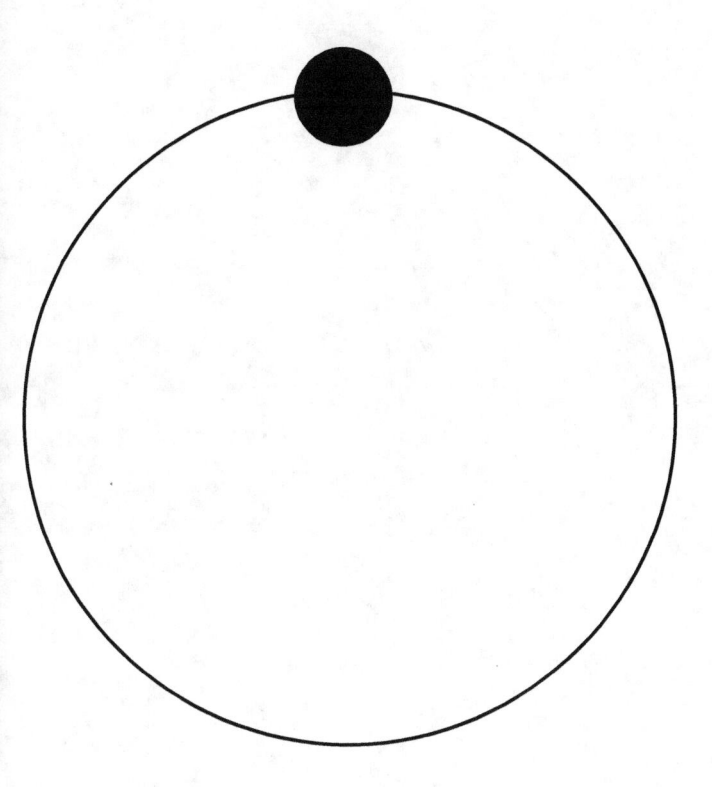

The Kiss* (2000)

o   o   o   o   o

F evered images of Obelisks* fluttered through my mind as the sky and laser-guided stars rolled away, the fading sounds of New Year's revelers growing distant in the night air. On the South Bank, I had leaned into her body beneath diamond-embedded fans scintillating in the soft bedroom light, blue walls shimmering wildly. We'd forgotten about the looming apocalypse within minutes of the new year dawning and spent the early morning hours fucking on a checkered carpet while I watched her fractured reflection in a cracked mirror. Purple hair and hazel eyes, alabaster skin and an inviting mouth... I slithered into the crystalline morning.

Trudging through the snow to the underground terminal, I saw zone posts being erected near the Picture Gardens, where trees and well-tended bushes laid quietly under a layer of frozen water crystals. About to descend onto the platform, two women in long winter coats stopped to smoke, their faces thin and bony, pale and breakable beneath the obscured winter sun. One of them had a black eye, and the other tried, unsuccessfully, to wipe the running mascara off her right cheek.

A temporary sign had been placed on the platform: *Leaving the Fifth Ring? Your status in the Sanctum has been revoked as of midnight, January 1st, 2000.*

The final divisions had permanently come into place overnight, only fourteen months since the last. They were a cold counterpoint to Aurora's warm and quivering flesh, which had quickly become my prison.

"What do you see when you sleep?"

I turned, and my gaze met Leon B.'s for the first time. We stared at each other in a way that defied interpretation—two pillars of skin and bone reaching across invisible barriers. I felt compelled to shake his hand, but neither of us moved. A feeling of dread crept over me; I sensed I had seen him before.

"Answer my question."

"Obelisks," I said.

Leon smiled.

"I've been dreaming of ice cream and butterflies, but I've also seen you. Many times, in fact. You pass through my dreams and attempt to evade me, but I'm persistent. I feel we're connected... Somehow. Now, here you are."

Glancing at my hands, I saw there was no blood on them. Breathing a sigh of relief, I sat on a bench. Leon stood over me, his slender fingers reaching into the pocket of his flowing black coat. He handed me a lead globe.

"Keep that. It will gain you access to the Inner Rings. There are no transports running today, so let's talk. I've been waiting for you."

He settled in beside me and placed his arm around my shoulders like we were lifelong friends.

"You're probably confused, which is fair considering we met only a moment ago, but trust me. You should talk to me about the dreams you've been having."

"How do you..."

"Know about your dreams? Don't be surprised. Everything will make sense in due time. It always does."

This is how it began; I'm not sure how it ended.

VHS Dream* (1995)

o o o o o

*D*ie Tür ist Zu—The door is closed, yes. All doors, all passages, will eventually be sealed. My past will melt like an Antarctic ice sheet. But... I could see *it*, deep in a crater, covered in the red dust, breathing. My mind hovered over it, and I imagined inhaling the alien ash like a fiend who sniffs cocaine off a tiny mirror, a dense flow of pleasure exploding the neurons, my astral body dancing outside its shell.

The comedown through the remote viewer lens ended with me vomiting black bile; I watched as it became bright yellow and orange. I saw her there—on the red planet—and then she was in my room, on the television... Her smooth thighs opened wide to reveal the blessed wound, a stream of blood and semen leaking onto the floor. I sat in the dark, smoking menthols with the window open, feeling the cool air crawl over my lizard skin. My mother always said she had given birth to a lizard.

I had popped a couple codeine pills; they marinated in a pool of stomach acid to the tune of Aurora's moans as I watched her get fucked over the edge of a sofa. Aurora, with one dilated pupil just like Ziggy.

She bit her bottom lip; my ejaculate hit the screen as she faked an orgasm.

The fragrant kitchen of desire—seduced by the sight of milk-white flesh and driven by the cool penumbra halo shimmering around her... Yes, that door is closed, but others open. Aurora, the garden path, the rose rising from the ashes of bleak days and nights.

Failure is a gift.

With blurred vision, I stood and looked into the heart of the burgeoning night, the artificial brilliance of LEDS grinding away past, present, and future possibilities: artificial light shining over smooth glass and empty faces, my potential washed away in the spectral glow. I turned off the tape. Actually, I paused it in mid-moan, then brushed my fingers over the frozen image, feeling the codeine seize my limbs.

Aurora didn't respond until I played the tape again. Eyes closed, she moaned and writhed as a man in a balaclava pounded her over and over—this time up from behind, up against a wall, his leathered hands wrapped around her throat. She told him to push harder and faster with a scowl on her reddened face, sweat dripping off her forehead.

My face was numb. As I blew the menthol smoke clouds around the room, I paused the tape again: Aurora with a leather finger in her mouth. I exhaled smoke at the television screen and the colours shifted, moving slowly like low rain clouds over the horizon. Everything felt white and dense, like packed snow over my limbs and face. I hit play once more and let the scene run its course. It ended with Aurora smiling at the camera and giving a little wave.

I imagined my hand running through her hair, the other gently moving over her taut stomach. I stared into the grey lines when the tape stopped.

ENTER THE CHAMELEONS (2000)

o o o o o

We met again on the second morning of the new year; the light was just beginning to swell behind the artificial tree line on the east end of the Picture Gardens. The frozen air numbed my lungs while my head hummed, as if it were on the brink of implosion. Leon B. stood idly by the entrance to a tunnel that led to the Fourth Ring, sealed off prior to the permanent partitions being erected. He flashed a smile and handed me a coffee.

"Lots of cream and sugar. Just what you need to bring in the new year."

I said nothing for a moment and turned my gaze to the cerulean sky, sipping coffee and revelling in the ambiance of the new year. Import, underground blend... Hard to get a hold of in the Fifth Ring.

I was probably still high from my fuck session with Aurora.

"I know what the fuck you do, man. I'm in the same business—the business of seeing past the walls, the buildings, the bullshit... A Prime Adept. I see what you see, and I saw your twisted face when I was in a coma from an overdose. We come from the same place."

I looked at him and laughed.

"What do you mean we come from the same place?"

With his hand, he motioned to the tunnel.

"Meet your brothers. They've been anxious to meet you."

Two men stepped out of the tunnel: one adjusting his sunglasses, the other inhaling what looked like concrete dust but was likely dream powder—it was becoming all the rage in the Fifth Ring. They resembled each other like twins, then resembled me, then resembled nothing.

Leon said, "We're in a New Age now, full of possibility, new realms... Take the leap with us. We'll make it to the other side."

"The other side of what?"

"What 'the other side' is there but the other side of death?"

They grinned in unison. Now the two men looked like Leon. I laughed again, finished my coffee, then followed them into the tunnel. The occasional row of lights illuminated our path, and as I walked, the space grew tighter—it was as though we were approaching the edge of a black hole. A small group of ants crawled over my feet. I thought about how, from their perspective, we would be like Gods, and the size of our planet would be the size of the Universe to them; they were crawling around in a minute space without knowing the true extent of the bubble... Leon saw me contemplating the insects at my feet and stepped on a few of them, grinding their bodies into the earth.

"The power of a God, my friend."

THE CAROUSEL (1996)

o   o   o   o   o

I would hang out at the carousel in an abandoned amusement park in the heart of the City (Sanctum), long before the Rings; the rust on the giant Ferris Wheel could be seen from a great distance.

After eating a handful of magic mushrooms, my head filled with colour. An old friend, long dead, had said, "Don't take them during the day, or the synergy with natural light will be too much." He was right. It would have been an overload to the senses, so I took them an hour before dusk. Late spring, already warm in the evenings—a cascade of fuzzy pleasures combined with the flickering lights around the park were enough to slide my mind into an upstream of pleasantness.

People often slept here, and on this night there were more souls than usual basking in the spectral glow of schizoid luminescence. Sitting by the carousel, hands deep in my leather jacket while watching the volcanic ash fall from my vapour-cig, the sky brightened as the psilocybin circulated through my veins. I crushed the cig with my alligator shoes, toxic fairy dust flitting into the air in tiny puffs.

Powering on the carousel, I climbed into one of the wooden cars adorned with old tags from phantom graffiti artists. Laughter turned to birdsong as the chemicals danced wildly in my brain, and I sat in the glowing centrifuge in the midst of a spinning world. The red planet, the phallic obelisk in the crater, Aurora twisting naked in the dust... I puked over the side, cackling and wondering when we would come face to face, when I would press my flesh into hers.

Passive dust and cloaked vagrants in cheap plastic masks. Inhaling vapours from smuggled dream caches. Even the 'shrooms had tasted tainted. My bleeding thoughts rotated as the bulbous strips of light passed by, pieces of black obsidian forming a mosaic of an electrified Northern Dawn. I separated the fragments in my mind by sheer will, feeling lighter than air.

The carousel stopped, the music fizzled out, and I attempted to shake myself back to reality. The LEDs buzzed loudly as I began to peak, and the pointed towers of the Sanctum in the distance made me think of Mars again. Aurora always seemed to greet me in my dreams, her phantom skin running over mine.

It felt like we were in a game of tug of war with each other, desperately trying to invade one another's minds across a huge gulf of space. Perhaps she wasn't real. Perhaps she was just a violent, sexual image created inside me to, ultimately, murder my body through the passivity of sleep. But...

The Sun rose over the amusement park, signalling that I had spent an entire evening chasing Aurora's image through the tunnels of my mind, madness flowing through my nerves.

The lights turned off and a voice reverberated through my skull, telling me: *Relax, let it flow, your death has already been achieved by letting go of your body.*

I stood and felt my bones crack and realign themselves, my lungs filling deeply with the cool morning air. On my way out of the park, I passed several dealers who were already soaking up the photons, ready to offer everyone a respite from their isolation and despair.

THE EFFECTS OF ISOLATION ON THE HUMAN PSYCHE* (1996)

○ ○ ○ ○ ○

Beams of light—thick, vibrant—passed by my face every time I was in the Chamber, my penis hardened by their radiance. I considered those experiences breakthroughs, callings to elevated sounds and vibrations where I could witness the Universe crumble and crack. My family thought I was making progress after nearly a decade of incoherent ramblings, mood swings, and excess of every kind. The mirror said otherwise, but my mind began to clear—or rather, it became embedded with a new kind of entertainment.

Aurora was beginning to fully form, coagulating when least expected.

There, in the miasma, I experienced the deeply sick side of myself: I felt a need to adorn myself in a horned skull and strip naked before running through the forest at high speeds, the blood pumping furiously in my chest while my face crumbled beneath violent frames of death. The edge of reason is where animal instinct becomes sharpened by the thrill of the hunt, imagined or not. My fantasies—recorded through a decade's worth of notebooks—encompassed a huge swath of those nights in the Chamber.

Who are your parents?—controlled images in the corners of my neural field—they even managed to crack smiles when I opened my eyes. The results were mixed. On the one hand, they appeared happy that I had shown signs of improvement. On the other, they were probably scared as fuck that I would try to kill myself. I couldn't begin to articulate the feeling of drifting to them; they were probably more lost than I was. Unlike my parents, I didn't care where my gruesome problems took me, simply because even the worst, most vicious experiences usually take us somewhere far more interesting— sometimes even showing us the path forward.

I would withdraw after the experiences in the Chamber, not out of fear or desperation, but for an opportunity to relive them outside that closed environment. My dreams were filled with the most horrific and beautiful scenes—splendid obsidian caves and deep blue ocean tides, coupled with rivers of run-off blood from sadistic wars. Dismembered bodies and lotus blossoms percolated in a mist of hot reds and oranges, the fallout from endless battles and executions. And yes, I would dream of Mars too, red and barren, inhabited only by my dark angel, Aurora, blowing me a kiss...

Take your medications. Swallow them this time. Don't you want to get better? I heard these phrases incessantly. "What does recovery even mean?" I would ask myself, going days in my closet without sleep while remote viewing hidden underground systems and stars, planets and dimensional portals. The mindstream flowed unabated through the aether, its current strengthened by sheer will. Sometimes I would blow a kiss back at Aurora, and she would catch it in her small, delicate hands. I imagined her index finger in my mouth—the same one she would masturbate with in those solo videos—the taste lingering on my tongue and at the back of my throat for an eternity.

I had agreed to give my notebooks to the group handling the Chamber experiments. I imagined their salivating mouths and rigid faces while they read my last digressions into mental hyperspace... Areas they would never see, hear, or taste themselves but had the audacity to make assumptions about on a regular basis. I told them repeatedly that I would disappear one day without notice, a reason to start anew. They didn't understand; frankly, I'm not sure if I did either, but one must listen to the clarion call in one's soul, even if it leads to a point of disintegration.

THE BLACK ROOM (1998)

○ ○ ○ ○ ○

We lit the candles together at Vespers in Section K, Block 1, Lot 56* of the Zone Temple, then went our separate ways down the hall, casually looking over our shoulders at each other like in a ridiculous rom-com. From my vantage point, I could see all the possibilities in her eyes, and they all led in the same direction: towards death. Nothing about that prospect bothered me in the slightest—I knew the age of chaos was dawning.

One night, after the Zone Priests had completed their daily ritual of opening the high windows to let our sins out on the stale air, we talked about the Tokyo Gas Attack while passing a contraband cigarette between us.

Aurora said, "One has to applaud the Aum Cult for pushing an apocalyptic vision on a mass of people. It is only in those frightful moments, when the elegant poem of death is spoken in someone's ear and they are desperately trying to save the pathetic life they have, that they are truly alive." I nodded in agreement—nothing she ever said dissatisfied me or rattled my emotions. We had actualized one another in disparate pockets of time and space; *this* is how I knew we would meet face-to-face, as impossible as it seemed, knowing full well both our minds were diseased. I imagined the Tokyo subway filled with sarin gas. People screaming and tripping over each other. Crying, frantic. Some victims vomiting, others dead... Yes. When one is facing imminent death, the mind is most active. The panic of the unknown comes rushing to the fore.

We finished the cigarette. Lit by the summer moonlight, she shed her top and placed my cold hands on her breasts. Aurora moved gently on my cock, the barest outline of her body morphing in the void.

I gripped her tightly as she moved her hips, my thoughts blending together as I came inside of her. She leaned in and whispered, "We are one."

When the whole world stands still, the demands of the mental space settle, leaving you adrift in the pocket of what some call divine love, its energy rising to infinite heights before dissipating in flakes of burned-out stars. Being inside Aurora—a part of Aurora—wasn't just pleasurable; it was also an attachment to a universal bond that would inevitably see us perish.

She brought her forehead down to mine. "Tell me what you see."

I spoke in a monotone, deeply, as though I were under the influence of dream dust.

"I see the curvature of the Earth. A thousand hydrogen bombs rain down from the upper atmosphere—a thousand Novaya Zemlyas explode in vast rings of radioactive light and consume the planet. I see the melted flesh of survivors set against a hostile sun gone black, but it's a future made brighter by the catastrophe."

She looked at me sadly and smiled.

"Don't die on me, okay? We have a long way to go together before it's all done."

I lifted her onto my face and drank her in, doubling the poison that had run through my veins since birth, her frozen image on the television screen dissolving through fantasy and onto my waiting mouth before cutting me open and climbing into my skin.

Ritual and Ideal (1999)

○ ○ ○ ○ ○

T he world, as it stands now, is an abbreviation—a small segment of a world that was once greater, more profound, gleaming...

I watched the dense December clouds release a soft trickle of blood. Maybe I wasn't the only one who could see it. The colour reminded me of the cryptic visions of Mars, and I stuck my tongue out to catch the droplets. The taste was mesmerizing; I dialed into my mind triangle. Manifesting the ballrooms of the red planet, I saw faceless astronauts mine craters and dissect the bloated corpses of their brethren, dead from mysterious ailments.

I could see it all. No one ever fucking believed me, but it didn't matter. The Zone Priests gave me pure psilocybin to enhance my attempts. I had thrown out all my prescription meds and nearly hanged myself within a few days of the onset of withdrawal, but that had passed. My mind was clear again, pure and bright like a chiselled diamond. The deep space reflections I was experiencing warmed my body. Aurora wasn't privy to my transformation; she had been moved up a level, her own treatment yielding stellar results.

We would see one another in the meeting hall—a dank, green tiled, badly lit corner of the Zone Temple that reminded me of cold days in an elementary school bathroom where my friends and I would chant, "Bloody Mary. Bloody Mary." At sunset, I would find Aurora alone at a window, studying a point on the horizon as though the setting sun were an out-of-control fire and she was contemplating the best way to put it out.

On this day, catching me out of the corner of her eye as I approached, she turned, a large smile forming on her lips before she spoke.

"We should fuck in space one day. On one of Jupiter's moons... Europa or Io. What do you think?"

I smirked while thinking about the boundary of her beautiful flesh and how, in this quiet and peaceful moment, I wanted to climb inside of her and disappear forever.

"Yes, we should do that. Somehow, some way..."

She placed her hand on my penis.

"Promise?"

I ran my index finger down her soft cheek.

"Of course. I don't break promises."

Aurora looked away and out the window, admiring the golden sunset in the West while lighting her fifth Astrum*. I followed her gaze, feeling a momentary peace before she put the Astrum between my lips and told me to inhale deeply. Within a handful of seconds, large hexagonal patterns appeared on my periphery; the hand Aurora had placed on my penis seemed to dissolve into me, touching my root chakra. I felt weightless, her eyes becoming nebulous pools of swirling dark energy, occasionally pulsing, reaching out.

"We're alone, except for the occasional camera recording our every movement..." She licked her lips. "Fuck. Take me right here as the sun sets."

Her words echoed in my head as our clothes floated to the floor, our bodies swelling with heat as I laid on top of her gingerly, conjoining our bodies like two entwined serpents.

22

THE POTION* (1997)

o o o o o

Jotenheim's Warehouse*, beyond the city limits, is where I entered the Reef for the first time with three women (think Macbeth, Act 1, Scene 1). Lounging about naked, high on mushroom tea, we laughed insanely. The warehouse was situated on a piece of abandoned land, far away from the chaosphere of the Ring. Here the locals consumed aphrodisiacs, fucking in a sea of sweat and semen, while casual observers on the sidelines taped the sessions for their own personal jack-offs. It was a place where those of us who were mentally off-grid went to indulge in each other's neuroses.

Everyone appeared strange, piercing me and negating me with their stares. Bodies everywhere quivered with orgasm, glimpsing the face of God for a few moments before becoming human again. A strict dress code was in effect: no rave pants, t-shirts, or bright colours—a great neutrality. The participants, mostly unclothed, stood in blatant contrast to the deep blues and oranges adorning the rooms where men and women alike were fucked in the ass and mouth with abandon. Screams mixed with grunts and moans, blood, piss, shit...

"Can I get you anything, or anyone?" a voice asked from behind me.

I turned, and a woman with purple hair and pierced nipples handed me a cocktail.

"I've seen you somewhere before, haven't I? You look familiar."

"Maybe you recognize my tits," she said, cupping them in her gloved hands.

"Can I have a taste?"

"Of course you can. This *is* the Reef, after all."

She placed two drops of a liquid on her nipple and leaned in. My tastebuds were flooded with sweetness as she forced me into her chest; I swallowed gleefully, not knowing what I had ingested. In the depths of the Reef, no one ever questioned what one saw or tasted, heard or smelled, for it took away from the mystery. I thanked her, then watched her fade away in the crowd of lost souls. Hands began to caress me, and my body trembled at their unfamiliar touch. I felt a sense of falling as flesh bonded with my flesh, the lights strobing hard and fast as I peaked. In the miasma of the experience, I pictured those warm hazel eyes, one iris larger than the other—wide and angelic, so well known to me, beckoning...

At some point I passed out, and when I awoke on the floor—it felt like days later—I was alone. Everything was clean and sanitized, leaving no indication of any transgressions. No evidence; only my naked body as a reference, proving nothing. I laughed for a solid minute before wandering out into the early morning, the cool air blowing me back into the city.

Within a week, I was in a psych ward.

The Oracle* (1995)

"Be a frequenter to lonely places." -Buddhist doctrine

o   o   o   o   o

Before the Rings came into existence, the Oracle lived in an old housing project used by the Orphic Doctors* and expelled initiates of the Zone Temple. I was the only one who ever saw the Oracle's face. In my observations, the temporal and physical worlds overlapped like layers of an onion.

I knew the way to the Oracle, but I didn't yet know why. A year before I was committed to the Chamber, the streets had pulsed with the air of death. Bands of industrial particles flitted and disappeared under the artificial lights like sparks from a crackling fire. I climbed countless flights of stairs to get to the Oracle's door; when I arrived, it shifted before my eyes, morphing into various intricate shapes. I knocked when it resembled a red rectangle, and entered before I received a response.

The Oracle, hooded and covered head to toe in a large black sheet, motioned for me to sit on a chair that was illuminated by a naked bulb of bright blue. Smoking in silence, I watched the walls ebb and flow in rhythm with my breathing. The Oracle spoke.

"I know why you're here; it's the same reason as everyone else. Only, no one has ever made it this far... You want to know the past, not the future. A past you cannot remember. Correct?"

I must have unconsciously mouthed *yes*.

The Oracle nodded.

"You'll meet her at various intervals; sometimes you'll know it, other times you won't. She's the active link, and you are the passive, dancing together."

25

I got up, snuffed out my cigarette, and watched the room start to liquify. A deep thrum emanating from the mouth (?) of the Oracle vibrated through me as I attempted to find the door I had entered; I grasped at empty space while the sound intensified. When my skull felt as though it were going to crack and spill my liquefied brain all over the shifting floor patterns, something extraordinary happened: a ring of light began to emanate from inside me, radiating outward in every direction—from the top of my head to the soles of my feet, to the tips of my fingers—spreading a loving energy before abruptly inverting and thickening into a feeling of utter despair and hopelessness. Tears crested as I looked at the Oracle's head.

"Always be prepared to die in forgotten spaces—left behind to disintegrate, only to be reborn in some other mode or form. Being afraid solves nothing; you have no choice in the matter anyway. This is the true mechanism."

On the ground floor of the dilapidated building, the sound of gunshots and fireworks being let off roused my senses. Reaching into my jacket pocket with a trembling hand, I grabbed my meds, placed them on my tongue, and struggled to swallow. I huddled in a corner, waiting for the stream of goodness to fill my neurons. A dirty clock on the wall had stopped at 10:10, probably eons before.

THE VISION* (1999)

○ ○ ○ ○ ○

At the tail end of spring, I had a vision of Golden Butterflies*, their wings casting off dust as explosions rang in the streets. Chlorine gas deaths, sniper kills, the muffled screams of murdered citizens... No one questioned the disintegration of property, the abandonment of families, or the senseless killings. The Age demanded blood; I just happened to witness its terrible dawning.

A coupling between two strange, hate-filled lovers conceived the Rings and all the intricacies of the frame that held them together, burning the retinas of the populace with neon oranges, blues and greens, the air nearest to the Hole* a mixture of chemicals, soot, and decaying flesh.

As the screams and death rattles calmed to a hum of dry extinction spasms, I took to the empty streets and followed the alleyways north, popping codeine without a destination in mind. Succumbing to pleasure, butterflies flashed in my periphery, flying into the Aurora Borealis.

"How beautiful," I muttered.

Death and resurrection always felt elsewhere, outside my personal scope, happening to bystanders who shouldn't have been there in the first place*. A series of forces acted upon my body as I sauntered away from the madness; the incessant murder drones continued until I was well out of earshot, and I sensed the codeine tracing its cool path through my veins. The sight of the golden butterflies coalesced with the opulent moon and the smell of dying lilacs, transporting me somewhere close to Paradise amid the increasing gunfire. Passing a phone booth, I heard a voice at the other end of the dangling receiver. I raised it to my ear and listened.

...who is doing this and why? That is the question no one is asking! Things just happen, and the world becomes smaller and smaller until we're all rounded up like cattle and sent to the slaughterhouse. Is that what you want your final moments to be? Wondering how the world got so FUCKED UP, right before some jack-booted soldier of fortune puts a bolt through your skull? Not me, not me! I would have to be fucking crazy to allow myself an End like that, but many will, and they'll have their corpses fucked for fun by the same people who killed them!

"Exactly! And people like us sound like the insane ones, right?"

The line went dead, and I let the dial tone echo through my head before replacing the receiver. I barely reacted to an explosion in the distance before continuing north, away from the streets of blood. Pulling the collar up on my jacket, I drifted into the industrial wasteland, revelling in the quiet embrace of the codeine as the butterflies continued to flit across my vision. The Aurora Borealis intensified.

"What a beautiful world."

THREE ABANDONED FILMS (2000)

o   o   o   o   o

L eon said, "Welcome Home!" so enthusiastically that I instantly felt at ease, even with a head full of dream powder* allowing me to forget how I got to where I was. He had led me to an expansive attic that overlooked the large industrial section of the Fifth Ring, his two assistants having casually vanished somewhere in the tunnel between the Rings. The room was spartan: a small sofa, a television, an antiquated VCR, and stacks of videotapes. Leon opened a glass canister and poured a dark pink liquid into a cup, downing it in one draught. His face became blue—*altered*— with a checkerboard pattern running from the base of his nose to the nape of his neck. He flashed a sparkling smile.

"I've been watching you through the lens of my mind. You've seen the Obelisk in the red dust too, haven't you?"

I turned away, answering haltingly.

"Yes... For quite some time... Along with..."

"Along with what?" he asked curiously.

"I'd prefer not to say, if that's all right."

"Of course," he said, waving a dissolving hand in the air. "Onto other matters, other *states*. There are some tapes I want you to watch with me: three lost treasures from before the Rings came into effect."

Suddenly I was on the sofa, but I couldn't recall moving in a *perfect* line from where I had been standing to the cushion. Leon sat smoking at the other end, *blue* smoke wafting from a cigar, his cracked lips blowing circles that followed each other in tight ovals.

The room throbbed with a blissfully bright orange; I was glued to the television screen.

"These gems were found at the bottom of that pile, left by the previous tenant. I am in awe of what they represent."

He pressed play, and the FBI warning truly felt sinister. My head swooned with *vertigo* as the glare from the screen exploded like a nuclear blast.

"The first film is called..."

His voice muted. I watched his lips mouth the title in slow motion, his face shimmering with a dreamy drug glow. Looking at Leon's shifting features, I felt as though he could read my thoughts through the heavy gauze of unfettered euphoria, as though he were passing his images of the red planet to me. I was elsewhere now, behind the mental curtain, hurtling at light speed toward my death. Then I heard Leon's voice.

"Mars is beautiful this time of year," he muttered. "The war in heaven is reflected in the war on this planet. As Above, So Below. You know what I'm saying?"

...mind split like a cleaved diamond.

THE GHOST (1995)

○ ○ ○ ○ ○

Premonition – precognition – sixth sense – Ajna: all are provocative terms for actually *seeing*.

My circulatory system was free of drugs other than name-brand pharmaceuticals with unpronounceable names. The pills were hard to swallow. I had been self-medicating in a rooming house deep in the valley, surrounded by trees and paths, not far from the cemetery of abandoned buildings and bomb shelters built for nuclear scares. The fear then—as it is now (?)—was of something over the horizon, transparent and elusive. I had a friend in that rooming house, Grace, who planted herself on the porch, drinking coffee and staring at the sky on clear nights. We had fucked a couple times under black light, hands pressed to each other's mouths.

I stepped out one evening during a new moon, waiting for the streetlights to come on, and she was there like she had been anticipating my arrival, smiling in the awkward way that people do when their minds have broken free from their bodies.

"Where are you headed tonight?"

"To the place the Oracle told me I should go."

"Who?"

"Nevermind."

As I walked away from her, she began a deep humming. An obscure hymn. Grace was fond of church songs, even though she was a fervent atheist. She said God had no place in an unfeeling Universe where the constants were battle and death. Sometimes she

31

would burn her arms with cigarettes to prove to me that no existent God would allow it. I'd nod in agreement, even though I felt she was wrong. Tonight, my walk down to the storm drain canal proved it. As my eyes adjusted to the fading light and the 50 milligrams of medical compound dissolved in my stomach, I saw her gliding barefoot across the surface of the water. Not Grace, but *her*... I tore at my face as Grace's hymn began to echo in the hallways of my mind, and my eyes watered with tears as I recalled the words of the Oracle.

I waved, and she smiled before dissolving in a cloud of angel dander over the muddied culvert. "Wild," I said. "Really fucking wild." At that moment, I confirmed the blossoming of my insanity. I stared at the swamp-like water, thinking the ripples were really just tiny distortions in time, spreading outward forever, touching nothing—the residue of a million possibilities. My body vibrating from the experience, I chuckled to myself as I stumbled my way back to the streets through the trees and bushes.

A cool breeze had come down into the valley. I spread my arms out wide, hoping it would somehow pick me up and whisk me away. It didn't, of course, and the unreasonable disappointment only served to depress me as the rooming house came back into view. Grace had disappeared from the steps—as a matter of fact, she had completely disappeared. A thin, emaciated young man known around the house as The Artist told me in measured words that "She just got up and left, saying fuck it." I went to her room, and her few possessions were gone. Oddly, the bed was neatly made.

Grace had vanished. All that remained of her was a skeleton of memories, shallowly buried in the killing fields of my mind. Rumours circulated around the house that she made it out of the Fifth Ring, and in my quietest moments, I wished her godspeed, wherever she laid her head...

Ramblings of a Mad Man (1998)

○ ○ ○ ○ ○

I would often go to a bluff near the South Bank and explore the abandoned houses that overlooked the valley. In the direction opposite the Sanctum was a three-storey Art Deco-inspired building where several hermits—former Zone Temple priests—lived and tended a small rose garden. The smell of hashish from their large hookah drifted down the empty boulevard. They had left the Temple out of fear: the Zone, with all its contrivances and all of its remnants, was a memory of a place forgotten, a displaced landscape burned from the minds of its inhabitants.

I may have been guided to them by the large streams of light I saw emanating from that area of the city. I had often asked people if they knew the source of the light, but they would look at me strangely and say they saw nothing. Their response only confirmed what I had always believed: I was within a mirage, a phantom zone... I had to laugh. A pull from my internal compass led me to a heavy wooden door engraved with sigils and symbols, a nervous energy sweeping over my skin when I knocked. I was greeted by several men in dark green robes who motioned for me to enter.

Without a word, they took me to the backyard, where the Patriarch of the Sacred Vedas* stared into a fire, his hands pressed together under his nose. He was clothed in a dark green robe emblazoned with a series of concentric circles over his heart, and motioned for me to take a seat across from him. Picking up a clay pipe, he took a mighty pull and exhaled a plume of spicy hash smoke.

"I suppose I could ask you if you know why you came here, but I believe I already know the answer to that," he said.

I remained mute because I sensed he could read my mind, peeling back layers until he got into the very centre of my fears and fantasies.

"You've come here out of curiosity, but you're also fearful of what you might find. Not only within the confines of this property, but also within your mind. Your experiences make no rational sense, and you lack the words to articulate them. You're likely on a cocktail of antidepressants or antipsychotics; all you really need is an injection of the natural into your life. The world is crumbling... This is why we took refuge here, on the other side of the river, away from the violence and chaos. I know what you dream of. It's the same thing we all dream of: obelisks and the womanly shape of Aurora."

I was stunned by his words, but I felt no need to react. My brain was spinning with paranoia; I felt as though he were probing my thoughts. A physical desire to run because of fear, out of the realization that I shared collective dreams with a bunch of narcotic-taking ascetics, was too much to bear. My mind in a frenzy, the Patriarch continued.

"In time, you will come to accept your place among us, but you need to get off that god-awful medication you're on. When the time comes, pay us another visit. We'll be back where we belong: in the Zone Temple. We expect you. We have all seen you before, unaware of our presence. Your focus is elsewhere, and that's likely where it needs to be."

"Where is that?"

"Obviously on the womanly form."

THE VOID* (2000)

o   o   o   o   o

Objects began to go missing—or at least they appeared to, the more time I spent in the presence of Leon. For a while, I thought that he was simply out to rob me, but I had nothing of intrinsic value. We spent the majority of our time in the attic, away from the madness of the streets, waxing philosophical, smoking and contemplating the many peaceful and perfect ways to end one's life.

Questions revolving around his appearance arose from time to time, and on a rare, oddly quiet evening, he revealed his story through a slurred, drug induced monologue. He had looked at the clock and laughed.

"Time really is a construct, isn't it? Meaningless in the sense that we derive no pleasure from it, only pain, knowing that on some level we only have a set amount of it. I overdosed a couple years ago and went into a coma; that's when I realized that time—as we perceive it—is meaningless. Also, something else happened... something far more intriguing on a quantum level. In my coma, I began to see faces, all unknown. I'd often see the activities they were involved in. That's when I saw you and her for the first time."

Everything froze when he said "her." His head was tilted over the back of the sofa, staring at the ceiling. Having taken some dream powder an hour before, my vision was clouding with deep, vibrant blues. I imagined Aurora straddling me as I laid my head onto her chest, but when I focused my vision, only a filthy attic wall stood in front of me.

"What do you know about Aurora, Leon?"

His stunted laughter echoed in my head. The dream powder worked its magic as he lifted his head and turned toward me, jaw slack, trying desperately to form sentences.

"She's not real, man. She's that image we all chase at some point in our lives when we're at our lowest point or some shit. Forget about all that. Move on. The chemistry in your head is all messed up, isn't it? I suppose all this dream powder isn't helping either."

"Fuck you. Of course she's real! I used to have pictures of her all over my bedroom wall. We're the same age... I even fucked her on New Year's Eve, didn't I tell you? We were in the Zone Temple together only a year ago! Don't be such an asshole."

This made him laugh even more, to a point where he could barely breathe. He managed to stand and grab a bottle of wine from a small cooler, pulling the cork out with his teeth. He tossed the cork. I watched strings of orange and purple trail behind it before it landed near my feet. I started to question Leon's sanity as the powder really took hold, and we slipped out of sync with one another.

"Forget everything you've been told. Surrender to the void, man. It's the only thing that's real, anyway. What you thought was fucking was probably you jerking off to a colourful movie going on in your head. It happens to the best of us. Concentrate on what else you've seen and what I've seen. Why do you think I wanted to find you?"

It was then, as he looked me directly in the EYE, that I pulled out a gun and shot him in the face.

THE LOOPHOLE* (1995)

○ ○ ○ ○ ○

Early November—the Taurid Meteor shower—a month of massive conjunctions and the first instance where I left my body. Projection became a regular event only after my initial breakdown just before Christmas, leaving me sedated well into the new year. Always the new year. Sometimes new beginnings, but often just endings. Codas to hopes and dreams that didn't come to fruition the year before: we pretend that we're better, stronger people once the cycle begins anew. The night of this projection, I had lain down quietly in the dark of the rooming house and soon found myself kissing the pallid stars, almost without effort.

I was in a tunnel of veils and date palms—mysterious and wet, unknown and bewitching. Hearing the breaking of waves and the melting of ancient ice floes... I was beyond normal vision, exiting Earth, going elsewhere—a loophole through the mundane. The comfort of feeling non-material was disrupted by the flesh.

I remember The Artist touching me with his cold, clammy hands, which was strange because my mind felt everywhere but in my body: pushing away from it, leaving it behind, hoping it would rot. An ambulance was called after my body shook violently and he screamed, waking the others in the house.

(The Artist later told me that he saw my body spasm and thought I had overdosed on a banned substance I must have smuggled into the house. I doubted his statement; I always closed my door at night.

In the summer, we'd often sit together in silence on the front porch. I think he kept quiet so he could hear the rhythm of the night, including the occasional far-off scream, while I'd sometimes think about popping his eyes out with a rusty spoon for interrupting my ascension. He eventually blew his head off in a ravine, recording his death amid sounds of gently running water and chirping insects.)

No one was ever going to believe it, I told myself, and no one did. They—the doctors, specialists, and family—looked at me with sorrow and expressions of puzzlement that betrayed what was likely going on in their own minds: *He's fucking crazy and probably needs electroshock.* Despite their thoughts, I felt incredibly lucid. Even the strangest of images and dimensional locales I headed through felt familiar and warm.

After his initial freak-out, he had videotaped and recorded my murmurings, which he left me as a final gift. He even wrapped the box in dark green tinsel and wrote "Merry Christmas" in a murderous script. One of the nurses told me he had dropped it off on Christmas Eve, just after my despondent parents had left to attend midnight mass and pray for my fractured soul. I couldn't move; or rather, I didn't want to move, as any movement would disturb the ultra-brightness of the chasm that had opened in my mind. After the lull and silence of Christmas Day, a series of doctors paid me a visit while I stared longingly at the gently falling snow.

"Beautiful, isn't it? The silence of this time of year is something magical."

I turned onto my back and looked at the doctor's face and the group standing behind him.

"I'm Doctor K—, and this is my team. We're going to get to know each other in the coming weeks."

"Not interested."

"You don't have a choice."

THE SPOILER* (1996)

○ ○ ○ ○ ○

I'd been there before—wherever *there* was—among all the other rejects. The only place open on the avenue was Fando and Lis, a hangout spot inside an old office building blessed by a group of people, similar to the Zone Priests, who practiced threshold magic. The sections of the building were developed in a circular design that led to a beautiful atrium at its hub. It was a kind of fortified Temporary Autonomous Zone* that dealt in obscure literature, golden praline eggs, and rare damask silk. A wide swath of people went through its doors, but not without being vetted upon entrance. Everyone was asked what they saw when they entered.

This question was a test, and luckily I was aware of the Fata Morgana in the entrance: a floating tapestry that depicted a demon piranha, a very realistic looking cat, and a child's Etch-a-Sketch. Perhaps due to the effects conjured by the group, any person leaving had no memory of ever having been there, except me (of course) and probably a handful of others. I knew Aurora had been there a number of times, and I felt lightheaded at the thought that we may have been in close proximity at some point. Her hair was shorter then, and she often wore discreet clothing and sunglasses while keeping to herself, basking in the preponderance of empty space above the atrium.

This time, upon entering, the strange aural sounds of Alvaro Pena-Rojas's "Drinking my own Sperm" reverberated through the halls while I looked for the nearest black market agent who wouldn't try to rip me off. It was rare to find one who was incorruptible in a place as lawless as Fando and Lis, but this mirrored what was happening in the outside world. The molasses-like trickle of time to the end of the millennium felt evident in every tense look, gesture, and movement. I always felt icy stares on me as I casually walked through the varied halls.

The familiar colours of the season—red, green, white—danced around me. Even the rejects who came to Fando and Lis felt compelled to celebrate the Saturnalian conception of capitalism disguised as Christ's birth. I had headphones on and was listening to a self-made tape of The Artist's death recordings and my freakout from the year before. Thinking about it, I could still feel the clammy hands of doctors holding me down as they shot me up with Thorazine... Ah, it didn't matter. I was clean of all that bad stuff, searching the sparkling halls for what I considered pure, finding it in the Atrium.

"You're looking for dream powder? Weed? As the old saying goes, I got it all."

The figure wore a silk mask that obscured their features to such a degree that I felt I was talking to an apparition. He (?) opened his (?) coat like a stereotypical drug dealer, revealing a plethora of illegal substances.

"I'll take a little weed and dream powder. Might as well give me a full ounce of each."

A light chuckle came from the figure's mouth, then I placed the payment in his gloved hand. I turned and started my walk back toward the main hall; the figure spoke in my direction.

"You know, this atrium is known to have strange effects on memory. No one ever seems to mention it at this time of year; it gets people kind of depressed. Then again, most of them don't remember anyway."

'84 PONTIAC DREAM (1997)

○ ○ ○ ○ ○

My first stay in the hospital was one of great insight—an opportunity to fine-tune the chaos under the influence of "better drugs." At least, that's how I recall those events, which means nothing. Memories are fluid; they distort and reshape as we drift further from their origin. Maybe it was all a fucking nightmare, but I don't think so: I remembered vague snippets of warehouses and embracing the violence inflicted upon smooth flesh.

At the hospital, an older man would stand next to me while we smoked outside, staring into the neon haze of the morning. He once told me, "They found you naked outside the city limits, bleeding and whacked out of your tree." How the fuck would he know? I had felt a desire to burn his face off with my cigarette, but I knew that would only create more problems.

It wasn't until after my release, weeks later, that I started having the dream: an '84 emerald green Pontiac Trans Am, driven by a woman in a black bodysuit, her head a mess of static-blurred features. I assumed that Aurora had slipped through the cracks of my unconscious and fit herself into all my repressed fantasies, mocking me from a distance as she sped off into the vaporwave dusk. The images looped over and over for weeks, and I felt as though I were deep in a fevered state from a familiar sickness. The rooming house was empty, with the exception of the few staff members who were supposed to prevent overdoses and suicide attempts. Obviously, they were not very diligent. Grace was gone, and The Artist was dead. The streets were becoming more dangerous so incrementally that one didn't notice unless their mind was attuned to the microshifts—and so many of us in that place were. That was our great problem: consciousness in all of its erratic, unpleasant glory.

Nights in the valley were lonely and reflective. I could often be found in the basement's small library, immersed in the dark, the hired help oblivious to what could be accomplished down there: hanging oneself from a bulkhead or filling a rotted brain with more knowledge. Lying on the floor, I imagined not having a body—all the rituals of the flesh abandoned for ghosthood, walking through walls and ignoring the confines of three-dimensional spaces...

It didn't take long before I felt a tight PVC skin against me as I tried to melt away, a great ball of static hovering over my head in that state of weightlessness. The static whispered to me in a tone born from the belly of a black hole: *Come see me outside; I'm waiting for you under the streetlights. Making me wait longer would be a sin.* When I awoke, the darkness felt as comfortable as it had during those days in the Chamber when I would be clamouring for the blinding light to touch me.

My body felt heavy as I lifted myself off the floor, disappointed that my spirit could not fully separate itself from the breathing meat sack.

Heart racing, my mind wandered—passing over the old cycle of dreams, reliving the sadness that crept into them when I watched the Trans Am drive off into the distance... It was a fitting reminder to never trust dreams; they only lead to disappointment in the end, just like all the other illusory factors of the universe. Placing my palm on the handle of the door, I paused, feeling the betrayal of the outside world. I creaked the portal open onto the porch, searching the street for any sign of life. Under the glow of the streetlight, an emerald green Trans Am was pulling away.

I screamed into the night sky.

DARK ROMANCE (2000)

○ ○ ○ ○ ○

A few days into the new year, I needed to find my way back to Aurora and her room with its concave mirror. Her building/love nest/sumptuous void made of onion stone blended into the frozen frame of the Picture Gardens, and in the early dusk of January it radiated a phantasmagoric haze reminiscent of Marienbad. Standing at the entrance in a body-length wool coat, her hair had already been changed to a bright orange. She wore tight black boots up to her knees, and a short pinstripe dress that showed off her milky thighs. We heard gunshots in the direction of the subway station; people had been trapped, like myself, in the Fifth Ring for days.

"You look different. It's your face or something."

I laughed.

"*I* look different? Your hair colour and wardrobe are never the same twice."

"You know the meeting between individuals is rarely the same twice. Every experience is unique. Isn't that wonderful? How many times have we met already?"

I didn't respond, as she was already standing in the dim foyer, waiting for me to follow her into the maze of unfamiliar hallways. She held the door open with her Left Hand sheathed in a red leather glove.

We kissed in the elevator, her body heat erasing any remnants of the outside air. Our elevator car ambled toward the heavens, her gloved hand caressing my face while my fingers weaved through the bright orange protein strands on her head. The light above us pulsed with a crimson glow, and she spoke softly in my ear.

"Where have you stayed these last few days, now that the Ring is closed?"

"I stayed with a friend who lives right on the edge of the Ring. I met him right after I left here. Now I'm back, and you..."

Her lips nestled into my neck, and I hit the emergency stop. No one would come to our rescue; neither of us wanted to be saved. The sight of Aurora's skin bathed in the bloody effulgence of our steel tomb seeded a question.

"Have you been haunting my dreams, Aurora?"

She was already on her knees. Our eyes locked deeply as she pulled out my stiffened member and ran her teeth along the shaft. Aurora did not intend to pleasure me. Her red-gloved hand squeezed my testes hard; I pulled on the handful of her hair in my fist. She laughed.

"Who do you think I am? I'm a figment of your imagination, out to do one thing..."

THE COLLECTOR (1995)

○ ○ ○ ○ ○

When the days felt too bright, long, and unbearable, I would find comfort in the War Room, a local lounge whose simple cuisine, marble torsos, and vaulted roof of glass and iron eased my mind. Far from decadent yet attracting a posh clientele, one could go there to decompress and have an oxygen cocktail as "Into the Fourth Dimension" played on the surround system. The owner—a former gambler—was behind the bar, smoking and drinking Mai Tais; he usually didn't have any night help. The evening I met The Collector, I had a spot near the back where I waited for him to appear with a suitcase full of black market videos. A man of punctuality, he arrived promptly, sat across from me, and ordered a glass of red wine. He had the borrowed flesh of a junkie, but he didn't use. A lifetime of dodging the law in an increasingly hostile world was enough to age a person, he'd said.

Peering at him intensely, I asked what he had for me. Shifting in his seat and looking over his shoulder, he opened the leather case to reveal a stack of imported VHS tapes. Cracking a smile, I reached for the pile like a greedy toddler.

"Ah, no touching until you cough up the cash. You know the rules, bro."

"How much for all of them? This is gonna set me back. Cut me a deal?"

"I cut you a deal on the last buy because I like you, but I've got bills to pay too, buddy. Besides, you should pay a little extra this time. I have a whole trilogy of bondage videos featuring that

Aurora I always hear you barking about. Should be worth your while if you're willing to be a nice guy, for once."

He showed me the video boxes wrapped in cellophane. Aurora's face—rouged and perfect—stared angrily at a bald servant who was licking the edge of her shining stiletto boot. My body felt the magnetic pull of her form dressed in the kinky armour of deep fantasy. The Collector slammed the briefcase shut.

"Last chance before the train departs, pal. You buying or not?"

"Of course I am! Was there ever any doubt?" I gave him a perverted wink and watched him slip the stack of bills into his coat.

He paused as he was about to stand, a quizzical look on his face.

"Are you interested in a little protection? You may have noticed the city is getting more wild by the day. We need to show all these weirdos who's boss, right?"

Reopening the briefcase, he showed me a nickel plated handgun nestled beside a full pack of live rounds and motioned for me to pick it up; I hadn't held a gun since I was a teenager hunting deer with my father in the hinterlands. The weight felt nicely balanced in my hand.

I placed it back in the case.

"How much do you want for it? I blew all my cash on those videotapes."

"Call it a feeling, a hunch, or a premonition, but I think that you're going to need it. No charge, my friend. Don't go around saying I'm not a nice guy, ya dig?"

THE OTHERS* (2000)

o o o o o

Time, as always, felt like it was running out. And of course it was, no matter what I may have wanted to think. In my case, it was running a little faster—just enough to increase my panic and anxiety to a level of constant tension. I could smell *them* after me—Leon's associates from places and parts unknown—ready to slit my throat because I had left a gaping, bloody hole in Leon's head. I needed pills, or dream powder, or even liquor to quell the taste of death in my mouth. However, when faced with the possibility of non-existence at the hands of strangers, the need for clarity trumped all else.

I travelled throughout the Fifth Ring looking for the tunnel that we had passed through on New Year's Day, the sweat on my brow mixing with the winter air.

I asked myself why I had shot him, and the answers I generated seemed simultaneously obvious and unreasonable. A natural first step inquiry was to wonder who he was and why he had been drawn to me, which led me to conclude that all the talk of his coma revelations was a put-on. But what the fuck did I know? My taste for mental chaos over the years had caused such a tear within me that the razor's edge between sanity and insanity was only a hair's breadth. I couldn't recall what I did with the gun, but I could hear The Collector's voice in my head say, "We need to show all these weirdos who's boss, right?" over and over and over, until I let out a scream in an alley so remote that even the rodents didn't stir.

Regaining my composure, I looked up from the piss-coloured

snow glowing sweetly under the LED lamps, and in the distance I saw the tunnel appear like a portal willed by a sorcerer—an event that couldn't be attributed to anything other than fate or luck.

Unlike the last time I had passed through the tunnel, the air was now fresh and the lighting was bright—almost cheerful—in contrast to the overcast winter sky that blanketed the city like an opaque sheet, smothering one's thoughts and greasing the depressive gears. Who would want to turn back, even if they didn't feel as though their life were suddenly tilting toward the grave? Aurora wouldn't turn back. At least, that's what I felt...

I wondered what would become of her once I passed through to the Fourth Ring.

Drawing closer to the end of the path, I could see the outline of two figures standing on the precipice of the Fourth Ring, waiting for me to exit the tunnel. Pausing at a considerable distance, I reached into the deep pockets of my overcoat and felt the smoothness of the lead globe that Leon had given me only days before. I continued toward them.

"Evading us is quite a difficult thing to do, and you didn't quite make it, did you?" one Twin said with a smirk.

Pulling out the globe, I handed it to the nearest Twin. He weighed it in his palm, then passed it to the other, who did the same. They looked at me in unison, then tossed it back to me. Stepping aside, they let me pass into the Fourth Ring, watching as I tossed the globe between my hands. "You're going to have to pay for what you did to Leon, you know," one of them yelled as I walked on, but I had already shut them out. My heartbeat quivered, and I knew I would never be the same again.

PART TWO

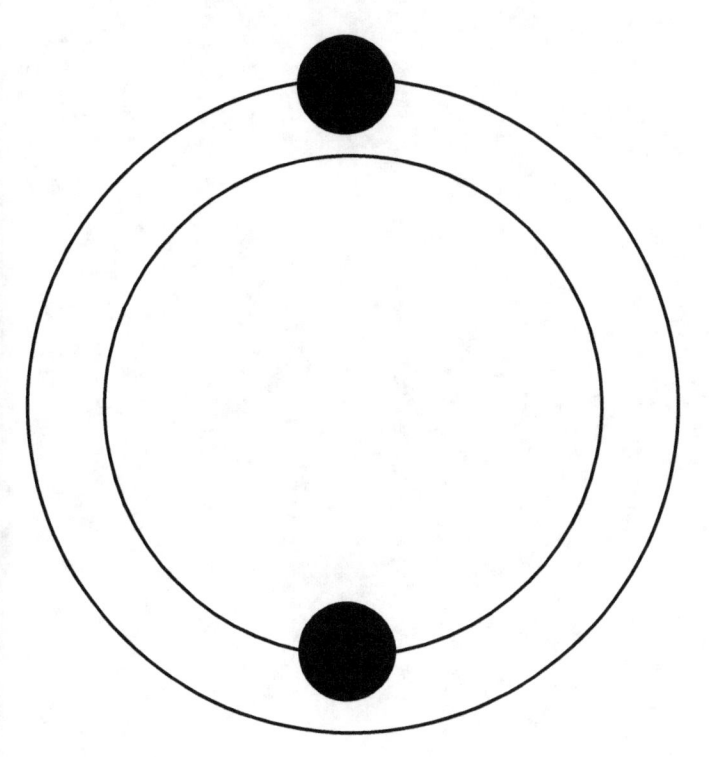

ILLUSION OF EGO

o o o o

DSM XV (Special Edition)
Temporal Disturbance Disorder

1. This condition exhibits a wide range of symptoms and manifests into full blown psychosis if left untreated. Patient may show the following in the early stages, particularly in adolescence:

    a. Feelings of "warping" through past, present and future time frames— all of which may be fantasy.

    b. Seeing "timelines" as well as tasting or hearing them in the form of synesthesia.

    c. Other auditory and visual hallucinations are present in 90% of cases.

2. This condition is also divided into two categories:

    a. Catatonic—patients feel perpetually suspended in a "warping" state.

    b. Highly focused but suffers from intense feelings of alienation from the general populace.

She hisses and swallows me. I have dissolved in the glowing warmth of her cleavage, naked and breathless, a chill racing over my skin as my penis deflates. Really, it's all a fabrication, a dream on speed; it rushes to the forefront of my mind before disintegrating.

I grasp at the fingers of the images, but they shrink and fade. Memories of ghosts and bitter days hover over the porticoes of the courtyard and the great bulls of Nineveh, reconstructed in tandem with the ungodly diversions of the Arcades. Perhaps she will try her best to reach me: push through the barrier and find my twitching limbs longing for her.

A voice I don't recognize whispers, "The Universe is an ocean of dazzling light, and on it dance the waves of life and death."

They see me grin but don't know why I do it. Maybe it's because—foolishly—I have hope. I carry scraps of her words with me, lovingly pressed to my chest as I try to sleep at night. I repeat them like mantras, over and over, until they become unconscious reflexes of my mind.

Alone in the aether, I am untethered, weary. I sing heretical hymns in the lost cathedral, unable to cleanse my bloodied halo; an acidic farewell to you burns my throat. I see you there, always, because that is where we fucked, in the Zone Temple...

Sitting on my bed overlooking the courtyard, I look out the window and watch the dull autumn sun peek over the horizon. I see a group of motionless people looking downcast into the earth and up into the heavens where no angels fly. The door to my spartan room opens, and in walks an unfamiliar man sporting a lab coat.

"You're awake! That's always a good sign. We thought we had lost you. How are you feeling today? Sluggish?"

I don't respond out of fear that the wrong words will incriminate me; he gazes into me with pale grey eyes, and words eventually form on my lips.

"I think I killed someone. Where? I don't know... It wasn't here. Do you know about this? Have I said this before?"

The doctor writes down everything I say. In defeat, I close my eyes, making the world disappear.

THE DEAD STAG

○ ○ ○ ○

I have no clear recollection of my Father's face—a shadow always seems to obscure his features when he appears in my dreams and in the rare instances when I think about my childhood, which feels like a billion lifetimes ago. What remains clear among all the blurred details are the occasions we slipped out of the city to hunt with a pair of rifles. He had learned his excellent marksmanship skills from my grandfather, who had been a sniper in a long forgotten skirmish or war. I never met him, as was the case with multiple people on both sides of my family; many had experienced premature death, including some who were murdered. Others simply went missing. The curse dealt by the Universe to my ancestors surely meant my bloodline would die out quickly.

Maybe it was this knowledge that pushed my Father and I to hunt—to pursue that road to the inevitable end, watching intently as life burned out in an animal's eyes. Father didn't see the killing of an animal as cruel or evil; rather, he perceived it as a creative process. Through enacting death, we, the hunters, were participants in the process of nourishing the earth with its desired flesh, ensuring that life would continue ad infinitum.

I killed my first stag in a picturesque clearing not far from where we had decided to camp. It was a beautiful creature, unaware of our presence. I lifted the rifle to my shoulder and aimed at its heart through the crosshairs. *Pull the trigger, son. You have him.* The blast echoed through the forest, and the stag slumped to the ground. We walked over to the carcass, and I looked into the noble animal's eyes like I was told, to see the fruit of our creative effort. I should have felt accomplished, proud even. Instead, all I wanted to do was skin the stag, adorn myself in his flesh, and don his skull and magnificent rack as my crown.

CRYSTAL AND DAGGER

o o o o

Numbed by a cocktail of prescription drugs, the nights pass slowly as I drift in and out of sleep. My blunted mind can barely conjure a cohesive image of Aurora; she has begun to fade from my dreams. The only pleasure afforded to me is masturbation, and it is while I am masturbating during one of these indescribably lonely nights that a miracle happens.

Placing my hand around my member, my easy breathing lulls me into a semi-conscious state. Slowly, the bends and curves of Aurora's body appear. I prolong my repressed ecstasy, wanting to drink in the image as much as possible before (hopefully) passing out. As I draw closer to orgasm, the door to my room is inched open by a nurse that I don't immediately recognize.

"Are you shivering? Do you need another blanket? Or... maybe a warm body by your side?"

I think I've misheard. Before I can respond, she steps into the low light that filters in from the courtyard—a pallid blue that seems impossible—and stands over my bed, a piece of rose quartz hanging from a silver chain nestled comfortably in her cleavage.

"Aurora? Is it really you? How did you get here? How did you leave the Fifth Ring?"

"It's a secret."

Climbing on top of me, she places her warm hands in mine and squeezes them hard to let me know she is real. I try to sit, but she releases my hands and places her palms on my cheeks, telling me to remain as I am. The subtle smell of hand cream and a sweet perfume are enough to euthanize me as she kisses my lips. The quartz dangles on my chest, my freed hands moving slowly down her back, pausing slightly on her buttocks, pushing her onto me.

All my prayers of desperation, all the tired, wasteful thoughts, evaporate beneath her touch and tongue as we tousle quietly in the bed, just like we did in the Zone Temple eons before. Every neuron in my brain is firing cleanly and without effort, and I find clarity through her touch. She lays beside me and nuzzles into my neck. It is in this moment that I snap back into the grim reality of my prison.

"How did you find me? I'm not even sure how I ended up here."

"I can sense you everywhere you go. I'll get you out of here, but it's going to take me some time. You'll have to be patient."

"Whatever you say, I believe it. Across all universes, I believe you, Aurora."

I feel the warmth of her body as I drift to sleep, but when I wake the next morning and see the same tired faces in the courtyard below me, I feel abandoned. As the day wears on, my faith increases, and though I no longer have the shrine of her body to worship at, I have a promise of absolute salvation to keep me awake.

A TRIBE FROM THE GHOST PLAINS

o   o   o   o

I had heard of the Plains tribe when I was young, though always in whispers or a derisory manner. When I first read about them in *A History of the Plains Tribe**, I learned of a People who were devoted to the visionary experience—a far cry from the stories in the city that pegged them as black magicians and primitive outcasts. In the second chapter of the book, I discovered an almost imperceptible thread...

The Plains Tribe—a People with absolute conviction about the interactions of the elements and their effect on the human mind—believed in the divinatory power of dreams and visions. So much so that all major decisions that may have affected the tribe were hoisted on the shaman, who was unafraid to cast himself before the harsh spirits in order to gain more wisdom and understanding. These practices were eventually co-opted by the priests of the Zone Temple, who spent many years in the tribe's company, learning the ways of medicinal herbs, sorcery, and fruitful dreaming.

The night after I killed the stag, I had fallen into a feverish state, at the mercy of odd dreams and delirium. It was the genesis of my disease, my reckless abandon into the void-shit of the coming years.

What is my disease? I don't even know. The well-dressed, clean shaven whitecoats won't tell me a thing. "Test Subject A" is what I've dubbed myself, but I've been a test subject since those nights when I first felt the thinning of the division between control and chaos. The world watches me unravel as I watch the world do the same, or something to that effect.

The horizon is clearing, and everything I observe outside my window reflects my newfound clarity. I stop taking my pills.

THE DRESS*

o   o   o   o

I have become a fixture in the courtyard, where I contemplate the series of events that have brought me here, finding solace in Aurora's promise of escape from the psychiatric panopticon. My lucidity makes me nervous and anxious. It's not safe to be this clear and certain in one's mind—abundant chaos inevitably falls in favour with chance, and on that true path is where events of significance lie. I don't fight the crystalline thoughts of normalcy, almost enjoying my vapid existence at the hands of my oppressors; they have no idea I have dismissed their cocktail and left their party.

The "drink this, it's good for you" type of talk follows me through the sanitized halls and into the open air, where the sky above the Fourth Ring resembles mouse hair, matching the heavy smoke from the cheap cigarettes that float around me. The other patients pay me no mind. Their issues don't cross over into my interpretation of reality, or mine into theirs. We are our own separate galaxies, simply nodding at one another from time to time before returning to the mud huts of our minds.

A package arrives. Fully inspected and laid open on my bed, a piece of thin wrapping paper covers the prize. I peel it back to reveal a neatly folded dress, which I lift out lovingly, like I am handling a newborn child. The expertly stitched, sun-yellow dress unfurls; I hold it up carefully, admiring the beautiful pleats, caressing the soft fabric. Laying it out on my bed, I imagine it hugging her hips, her breasts filling the bodice, her dilated pupil never shifting, as though she is inviting me into her body through the lens of her soul.

I examine it for a long time before stripping naked and slipping the garment over my flesh, revelling in its softness against my rough skin, imagining the whole of my being inside Aurora's through the tactile sensation of the elegant fabric. Reclining on my bed, I press the silent call button to summon a nurse. One of the regular, nondescript males enters and quietly asks what I need.

"I need to be shaved. All my body hair must be removed. Immediately."

With a subtle smirk, he departs to prepare for what is going to be a lengthy task. Two different nurses enter the room and say I will need a calming injection; they don't trust me to remain docile.

"I assure you, I'm already dead. Nothing more can be done on that front, wouldn't you say?"

No response, just the pin prick of the needle in muscle tissue and a gradual descent into the netherworld of drug fog mixed with the slight tug and drag of blades over my body. Slipping further down the spiral of intoxication, I hear Aurora's voice call out to me from somewhere, like she is speaking from the bottom of a staircase, urging me along... *Our home awaits, after the marriage... Carry me—all of me— through to another life.*

Through the fuzz, I hear one of the nurses say I will need to remove the dress.

All I can mumble is, "The dress stays on."

BETTER LIVING THROUGH CHEMISTRY

o   o   o   o

"Swallow your thoughts of her. She is not real, and she couldn't have gotten in here like you say she did... I think that you may need an adjustment to your medication. How would you feel about that? Are you experiencing any anxiety?"

Dr. K— and I sit in near darkness for an hour before he decides to turn on a small lamp in the corner of my room, bringing a modicum of brightness into my private world that craves only Aurora's presence. Sensing my thoughts like the demonic ghoul he is, he says her name in a tone I do not appreciate—one of condescension, almost revulsion.

"Who or what is this 'Aurora' delusion of yours? Can you explain it in simple terms? Maybe then we can lay the matter to rest and focus on getting you back on your feet, out into the wider world."

During an hour of stunted conversation, the dress has not been mentioned. In his furrowed brow and empty expressions, I can see that he is readying himself to broach the subject, knowing that I will lay out my experiences like a blanket and smother his smug face in their truth.

He asks me if I smoke.

"Occasionally. Though, aren't we in a hospital? Isn't that forbidden?"

"You would think so, but exceptions can be made from time to time for interesting characters like you."

He hands me a cigarette, and I put the stick in my mouth,

lighting it with his gold-plated Zippo. After a few puffs, I recline on my bed and wait for him to attempt, in vain, to discredit me. His discomfort is palpable by this point, so I prod him.

"You haven't asked me about the dress yet, which is strange since it falls directly in line with what I've been saying," I scoff. "You should see the look on your face."

"So, why are you wearing the dress?" he asks dryly.

"We've been over this already, haven't we? Aurora sent it to me so I could have her close without her actually being here, and she came from the Fifth Ring into this hospital, in the middle of the night, to talk to me. I wear this dress to feel her presence. What's the issue?"

Pulling out his notepad, he scribbles furiously between drags from his cigarette, wearing an expression that betrays his demeanour. He looks satisfied, as though he's gained the upper hand on the nature of my mental state.

"As of tomorrow, you'll be moved to our isolation wing in Level Z, where your medication will be adjusted. Further therapeutic methods will be administered over the coming weeks."

I ash out the cigarette on the windowpane and smile into the darkness, knowing Aurora will find me—a warm Angel floating through the walls of cold madness.

THE REMOTE VIEWER

o   o   o   o

T he isolation wing is a blank, dismal menagerie of the
  enlightened. A broad spectrum of minds in this section of
the hospital are left to rot and atrophy under the false auspices of
creating better health for all; in reality, it only serves to stifle the
inner reflections and revelations of those same minds that the face
of the world scowls at each passing day. But, in my case, I had
planted myself firmly in the outer realms long before.

My calmness and poise surprise me as I drift into my natural
state. Beyond all the screams, rants, and other nocturnal ramblings,
I find my sacred space within the cavity of the bright palace
between my eyebrows, the mind's eye scanning the surface of the
red planet before settling on the firmness of the Earth that was alive
somewhere beneath my feet.

I often sit cross-legged on the floor, deep in reverie, seeing
objects and people unfamiliar to me: I disappear into the depths of
my mind space. I reach Aurora again, her body covered in silver and
gold as though she is ready to pupate into a magnificent life-sized
butterfly... She writhes on her checkered carpet floor, below a
concave mirror, slowly twisting and turning—her shape continu-
ously morphing through muscle contractions and stretches—until
she lays herself flat and purses her lips across the aether.

Always with the kisses, ready to liberate me at any minute—or
so I hope, even though I know my sentence beneath the thumb of
the good doctor has only just begun. He finds great delight in trying
to dig into me, usually as I dwell in deep absorption, ready with his

notepad and tape recorder. Strangely, I have little desire to strangle and disfigure him, despite the fact that I can smell the odour of death that stalks him.

His voice usually comes in through the wall speaker—he rarely has the courage to come face-to-face with me. He makes grandiose statements that, in retrospect, may have an ounce of truth to them. Once, while I was remote viewing, he commented, "You display incredible lucidity, considering the strangeness and chaos of your behaviour. I've had moments where I believed this all to be theatre that you're creating for your own amusement, though the incidents from the past would seem to indicate otherwise."

How does he have access to all my previous information, I wonder? Even the most sensitive documentation from the Chamber must be lurking around in the hollow of his mind, trying hard to get out through his gaping jaw. Do I not remember him from some other time, from another place I only glimpsed during a total deviation from my senses? Is he a potential enemy to be annihilated by the Angel named Aurora?

"I'm going to conduct a series of experiments with you because I can't shake how fascinating your condition is. You are truly one of a kind at this hospital, and because of that, I've been given some leeway in getting to the bottom of what might be ailing you."

"Nothing ails me. It's a twisted gift that was bestowed upon me, whatever *it* may be."

"Don't you know what afflicts you?" His voice crackles through the speaker.

"No, and it doesn't matter because my Angel is coming to free me soon. To free me from all of this."

MEDITATION ON VIOLENCE

o   o   o   o

At night, in my windowless, locked room in the basement of the hospital, I often feel the sting of long suppressed memories; they hardly feel real. As more details surface, heavy emotions bubble from the depths: anger and revulsion seep into my muscles, and I throw punches in the dark, chewing on my knuckles until they bleed. These masochistic acts attract the attention of Dr. K—, his nasal voice descending on me during moments of my greatest fury.

"You appear to be reverting to a child-like state. I'm afraid we'll have to sedate you before we can go any further with this study and treatment."

As his voice resonates through my brain, the door is unlocked by two orderlies—large, brutish men who thrive on the opportunity to watch us struggle in their massive, meaty hands. While I've been battling my memories in the dark, I've also been formulating my attacks. I know they will depress a syringe full of sedatives into my veins. The first man enters, and I manage to leap at him quickly enough to ram my thumbs into his eye sockets; the soft bulbs pop, the blood flows, and he screams in agony.

The second orderly is consumed with adrenaline and rage—unfocused, ill-prepared. I snatch the needle from the first victim and jab it into his neck. I watch him collapse to the floor, then I beat his face to a point where the bones shatter beneath the weight and force of my fists, already bloodied from my own indulgences. An audible gasp comes through the loudspeaker, and I hear a flurry of footsteps race down the hall.

In the brief interval before the onslaught of security arrives, I am mentally transported back to my time in the Fifth Ring. I hear the shouting and riotous death that consume everything there, including a sense of hope. The tunnel that led back to an old Self, old dreams and old experiences, feels enticing and fuels the task at hand: the obliteration of my oppressors. I lap at the blood on my hands and sit on my haunches in the far corner of the room, away from the door, poised to spring on my enemies the second they arrive with their batons.

Three guards storm in, brandishing their weapons, ready to obliterate. As I ram my head into the crotch of the first, I feel a heavy blow to the side of my chest and howl in pain. Cracked ribs. I pull the baton from his hands just as two others grab hold of my legs. Swinging wildly, I hit one in the face, splitting his cheek open, breaking his jaw. One leg freed, I kick the other's mouth with the heel of my foot, leaving him spitting split shards of teeth. In these few seconds, the first guard has recovered enough to grab a fallen baton. We square off as the others lay hemorrhaging on the cold floor.

I haven't noticed the fourth guard enter, wielding a taser. A current seizes my body. Images of previous incarcerations skid across my inner vision, collapsing slowly as my limbs go numb —blood everywhere. I start to lose consciousness; feeling the world slip away (as it always seems to do), I hear the crackling, nasal voice of Dr. K— tell the guards to quickly sedate me.

I am mummified and taken even further below the earth to a level only experienced by a handful of others. It is here that I enter my chrysalis and await Aurora.

From an Abandoned Work

o   o   o   o

None of the subjects who were held in Level Z—four total
over the course of the program—survived the final stage,
due perhaps to a total sense deprivation, leading to
dissociative reactions, insomnia, and starvation. My
research into the reactions that stemmed from these
extreme, unethical methods is, for the time being, a
matter of unofficial record and will remain as such
until any evidence regarding the program is ultimately
destroyed. Level Z, like the letter itself implies, is
the Endpoint, the coda to a dream I had where I could
finally bridge the gap between science and mysticism:
render the body useless in order to free the mind and
ultimately prove that what we see inside us is not just
an organic construct. Subject A showed the most promise.
After one hundred days entombed under those less than
ideal conditions, they entered a catatonic state. After
a slow stimulus increase over several weeks, Subject A
revealed that at certain points, time and space no
longer existed in the traditional sense, stating that it
was indeed possible to see and experience objects,
locations, etc. Subject A died of a stroke. The body was
incinerated, and the remaining ash was disposed of
entirely. Subjects B & C were entombed together. The
intent was to see if there could be dissociative
communication between two different consciousnesses.
Subject C expired only twenty days into the experiment,
while Subject B later reported—after stimulus therapy—
that Subject C's "spirit" stayed attached to the corpse
for forty days before departing.

Subject B's fate was a stolen scalpel across the throat. Like Subject A, their bodies were incinerated and the ash disposed of completely. Subject D's story, though interesting, is one that I have left out of this scientific narrative for personal reasons. Suffice to say, my direct involvement with this subject led to their death. This statement in itself is too revealing, but as the old saying goes, the devil is in the details, and those details will forever hover at the back of my mind, never touching the edges of the light. As to the future of this program, I feel confident that even through the process of death, a life affirming force will spring from the earth.

RITUAL IN TRANSFIGURED TIME

○　○　○　○

Waking up with a sense of disembodiment is not a new experience, though in Level Z, away from prying eyes, I undergo a more pronounced detachment from within my truth cocoon; it is deeper, more dense, further removed from the dimensions of conventional space... All that remains of my Self melts away, scrubbed clean from the face of reality. The precipice that separates the world of order from that of chaos has a width of a hair's breadth, and I slip into the quantum realm easily.

A series of tubes have been attached to me so I can excrete my waste and absorb nutrients. Other than the vague sensation of having plastic inside my body, my transformation is nearly complete. Soon I will have wings. I will traverse every wall with my Saviour. To ensure her arrival, I begin a series of mental rituals that I learned while spending time with the Zone Temple priests on the South Bank. Preparations for what they called "The Final Absorption" are laid out like a blueprint on the surface of my mind, objects positioned definitively in the appropriate place, each representing an aspect of the past, present, or future.

I bring forth the clearest, purest mental image of a candle, lit and unlit, whole, liquefied, in virtually every form I can imagine, so as to know it thoroughly. The next step is to break the image down into its constituent parts, then examine those parts until only the essence of the candle remains. I don't know how many days I feed energy into the image of the candle, but embracing its qualities is the easiest part of the whole process.

The second object is the dress, the fabric that clings to my body passively while possessing an uncanny power over me. Why is it that the objects of the present only gain power over one's consciousness as time passes into the future, and when we reflect back on them, the nostalgic seed sends its power to the past? Penetrating the image is difficult; I break it down until it is simply atoms that arouse me from my concentration. I permit myself a few moments to feel the restrictions of my body in my cocoon.

The line between waking and sleep thins as the days and nights wear on, until the distinction between those two markers of time becomes a superfluous concept. For an object of the future, I want to remember Aurora's face. The summation of my joy in a fractured world consists only of her features; it is a world impossible for me to comprehend, even at the best of times.

The final step is to visualize all three objects simultaneously in order to have a clear sense of where they stand in relation to myself before I banish them, further imprinting them into the deepest part of my consciousness.

Voices begin to crowd my inner space. My breathing slows even more as days blend into weeks. I can feel the end coming, the last vestiges of my ego wasting away with my body... Aurora's body melds with mine, seeping into me like water into sand; we are indistinguishable from one another.

At last.

Sun, Moon, & Herbs

○   ○   ○   ○

Exiting the cocoon and returning to stimulus sets my mind back a thousand years, partially unravelling the concentrated work I have done, but my thoughts of the Zone Priests remain. They spoke of a pure dream powder, more powerful in its natural state than any derivative. Rather than a typical high of elation and mild hallucination, the pure powder completely altered the user's concept of reality. The local dealers could only imagine having something that powerful in their arsenal to keep people coming back for more.

My mind palace glistens with a list of active substances that correspond to the planets. As I recall them, one by one, the words become rotating globes in perpetual orbit.

Dr. K— has no true conception of what he has done to my mind. I am those substances without form, sensing their qualities as they become me and I become them, coagulating then extending outward, though no one but myself can see it. Tethered to Aurora, the Sun and Son, daughter, lover... Her voice reads the correspondences to me from the centre of my pineal gland.

Ten parts Gold is equal to ten parts hibiscus. Ten parts Silver is equal to ten parts chamomile. Five parts Copper is equal to five parts jasmine. Two parts Tin is equal to two parts mint. Two parts Lead is equal to two parts cannabis. One part Iron is equal to one part ginger. Five parts Mercury is equal to five parts cassia...

My low whisper of the formula is likely viewed as nonsensical muttering by the doctor and his faithful. No one truly wants to witness the mind at work—watch it spew strands of the gross and fine, see all the obsessions, murderous thoughts, and bizarre behaviour come to life in radiant colour.

THE TRIANGLE

o   o   o   o

My eyes burn for a long time upon my re-emergence from imposed solitude, furthering a mistrust of light that has always existed within me, even during those days when Aurora was nothing more than a series of pixels on a screen. Breathing her into life and actually *feeling* her presence has awakened a swirling, dense mass of energy that, over time, has taken my shape. Looking at my reflection in a glass of water, the urge to meld with her assumes an even greater power.

Dr. K— plays an unsuspecting role in my total acceptance of Aurora. His ugly, clearly logical, unfeeling intellect has the sole aim of dissecting and interpreting the bright chasm inside of me, but it only serves to fortify my feelings for her in the deepest way. I know that from beyond the concrete walls of the hospital, my Self disintegrates in favour of Aurora's essence, animalistic and pure.

Dr. K— can feel the germination of something within me, which leads him to question me on an increasingly deeper level while I remain in a stimulated state. We speak with one another several times through a pane of glass. I understand his reservations and motivations for talking to me through a barrier, considering I have critically injured his staff. I can still feel the ghost current of electricity hover across my skin...

Looking through the glass a final time, a sense of pride flits across his face.

"Prior to your incarceration in Level Z, you demonstrated a reversion to an animal-like state. You seem perfectly calm now. Are you?" He smiles wryly.

"Calm is a relative term, doctor. If anything, my soul is so lightly weighted down that a simple stream of cool air will lift me from this malaise. When one foresees the conclusion to a story, there is a wild, chaotic energy that builds in anticipation of the ending. This is what is occurring within me. I've seen the end; now I'm waiting for it to happen."

Dr. K— chuckles lightly and shuffles some papers before lighting a cigarette.

"The only 'end' you're going to experience may come in the form of your physical demise once this series of experiments is completed. I have to be blunt: there have been others who have not survived, and you may not survive either. *How* is all of this ethical? You know our world, in its quest for the limits of knowledge, often bypasses what is ethical and moral. Consider yourself a part of this process, no matter the outcome."

I laugh uncontrollably. I let every atom in my body feel the vibration of impending freedom, away from all the restrictions of physical matter, the inevitable drift of time carrying me to the goal without any effort on my part. Dr. K— attempts to interrupt my mirth; he desperately tries to penetrate the glass with his nasal voice to catch my attention. I ignore his efforts and fall silent, shutting my eyes and folding my legs in front of me. I can still hear him: he has succumbed to his own aggression and is hitting the glass with his fists. The pounding ceases. I slowly open my eyes. Beads of sweat have formed on the doctor's brow, his chest heaving from a lack of oxygen.

"Relax, doctor. Soon you will understand your role in this blessed triangle."

THE END*

o o o o

At a precise moment during my confinement in Level Z, I give up any lingering scraps of monochromatic time by easing into the ever-present land of recurrence. I can't be certain—then or ever—of my position in the moving stream. Aurora remains the only constant, so I intensify my focus on her changing image in the magic window behind my eyes. I see her as a young girl and an old woman, hair cropped short with flowing locks in a variety of colours. As twins and triplets, as a ball of crystal, an emerald, a ruby... ever-present, though also distant, warm and cold and lifeless, bringing me sadness as I listen to the cries and whimpers of the others above me.

Dr. K— has not made an appearance in days. I try to forget his face, his sudden anger and loss of professional control, but then I realize he is simply a madman like me. Only, he is on the other side of the glass, staring at what he wishes he could be or, at the very least, detests. My thoughts of the doctor recede, and I hear a large crash on the floor above me—as though the weight of an elephant has fallen on the floor—followed by a series of screams.

Soon my ears are flooded by muffled voices, and the sound of chaotic movement rattles the walls. I jump up when the lights flicker. The glass partition shakes and reveals the face of a young man I have seen wandering the halls. With a grin as wide as a canyon, he pauses for a moment to mouth, "We're free..." Pressing my face to the glass, I try to see into the hallway a little better, the lighting outside flickering madly. With each passing moment, more patients trickle by, looking for an escape from the confines of Level Z.

My breathing slows as I realize what is happening: Aurora has come. Alarms sound as the noise and violence increase, but I wait patiently, longing for her shapely shadow and the gleam in her eyes. The body of a guard falls across the threshold of my door; his face caved in from a massive blow, the blood creates a crimson pool that inches back into the hallway.

In the flickering light, I see the head of the doctor peer around the corner, his hair gripped by a leather gloved hand, his eyes rigid with fear—urine trailing down his leg, mixing with the blood on the floor. Aurora is a vision of what I have seen inside myself: her hair is short, dyed an emerald green, and her dilated eye is ruby red. Every aspect is mixed and resplendent to perfection. Holding a pistol to the doctor's temple, she looks at me carefully as though studying a statue. She winks.

"I told you I would come, and I brought our friend. There's quite the party outside this room! Let's make this quick."

The doctor's trembling hand opens my cell door. I step out; she presses the pistol harder into his skull while tightening the grip on his hair. He is her only focus as I place my arms gently around her neck, but she nuzzles her cheek into mine before pulling the trigger, splattering Dr. K—'s grey matter all over the wall. I don't flinch at the sight or react to the pandemonium around us. Aurora grabs me by the hand.

"Time to make our exit—we have to hurry."

A FRAGMENTED LINE

o o o o

T he Fourth Ring falls into the background as we run south into a maze of industrial land claims. Aurora hasn't let go of my hand since we made our way out of the hospital, and as the chaos of the past hour fades from view, I find myself staring at the chipped black polish that adorns her slender fingers. We stop in a doorway to catch our breath, then lose it once more when we press our lips together. Drops of blood from Dr K—'s head are scattered over her face and clothes like a thousand freckles—reminders of an irreversible act. We are the hunted, but I can sense by the urgency of her kisses that she is prepared for anything, ready to cast off her sense of calm resolve with a moment's notice.

"I felt your presence while I was in Level Z, but there were a handful of times when I thought you wouldn't come. It was as though there was a blockage preventing you from shattering the walls and finding me. I suspect Level Z had some sort of protective barrier that prevented my escape."

Aurora isn't listening. Her thoughts are elsewhere, beyond the doorway in which we stand. She grabs my hand again. We continue to move south, into unfamiliar areas and streets that all resemble each other. Aurora knows the precise route as she leads us to the edges of the Fourth Ring. We settle in the attic of an abandoned warehouse under the auspicious light of the full moon. I haven't noticed the transition from day to night, but my body feels fatigued. I stretch out on the floor, and Aurora, straddling me, finally speaks.

"I have a place in the Third Ring we need to get to. We'll be safe there if we remain inconspicuous."

"In the Third Ring? No one has been there in a decade... How do you travel between the Rings???"

She presses a finger to my lips, then shifts her weight forward to whisper into my ear.

"You've been doing it too. We've travelled great distances together... It feels like a million lifetimes, and maybe it has been; there is a shift occurring, a fracture that cannot be repaired."

Her delicate face hovers above mine, displaying a sense of tension and worry. Aurora's arms tremble a little; a single tear runs down her cheek and onto my chest.

"What do you mean by 'a fracture that cannot be repaired'? I'm so confused. Why did you come back for me, then? What the fuck, Aurora."

Jumping off me, she presses herself against the wall. She throws her head back, then stares at the ceiling, searching for the right words to express her anguish. I don't move—I am paralyzed by her sudden rush of fear, especially considering she had so calmly turned the doctor into an apparition. The entire situation only serves to increase my anxiety as my mind begins to cloud once more. I look at Aurora, and she appears almost transparent. She speaks slowly.

"Come over and touch me; I need to know that you're still here and not a..."

THE SIMORGH SLEEPS ON VELVET TONGUES

○ ○ ○ ○

We are never bashful in front of one another; the pieces of clothing come off in a flurry. I bury my face between her breasts—they carry the odour of blood and sweet perfume, a dialectic I long to lose myself in as the night grows heavy and silent. Her fingers tug at my hair while my cold hands run over her warm back before unclasping a satin bra decorated with tiny M-16s firing stars from the barrel.

Our bodies become intertwined, lost and indistinguishable, and the full spectrum of our time together flashes before my eyes, beginning with my delusional fantasies that have been fed by images of her on a television screen; I had watched in erotic rapture every day before bringing her to life through furious hand fucking. The coming millennium gave birth to an impossible dream when I touched her for the first time; my emotions are heavy and blurred as my fast-moving thoughts turn to soft kisses on her lips and neck.

Our bodies meld in the dust—her cheeks flushed, hair wild—her fingers clutch my throat as I press my own into her soft, malleable breasts, wishing to savagely tear her apart and cannibalize her. *Make her mine forever,* I think. *There is no other way forward... We're in danger.*

"This will be the last time," she says breathlessly, reading my thoughts.

The violent heat from her thighs increases as we grip each other harder—in horror, in pain, in pleasure—nearly destroying one another in the process, muffling each other's mouths like we did during those nights in the Zone Temple, which hardly seem real.

Eventually it all stops; there is a complete arrest of movement and sound. For a moment, we are the only two people left on the barren Earth, together but apart, across a thousand memories and landscapes, broken dreams, and hollow endings to lives that have led us to this moment. Considering we are on the edge of the Third Ring, I know the chances of death are high. I have to pause, imagining the possibility of an untimely end, even if it is with Aurora at my side.

Aurora sees the passion drain from my face. She kisses my eyelids before sliding her body off mine, then lays on the attic floor like a corpse. I slip my arm under her neck, bringing her closer to me for fear of her fading from view. We turn to look at one another; our expressions are stilted, cold.

"Have you ever been beyond the Fourth Ring?" she asks in a whisper.

"No. Though... Some friends of mine found a way into the Third Ring years ago, but they never came back. Their families didn't file any reports or anything, they just accepted the fact that they'd never return."

"Have you ever wondered why they never came back? Were you ever curious? Because soon you'll know why."

A cold kiss, a quick redressing. We are gone again—back into the silent scream of the world.

THE CODE*

o o o o

Across cracked sidewalks, deserted lots, and dozens of empty buildings, a narrow path ambles toward the choked, black river. The Sun has begun its usual tired ascent on the horizon as we settle into a corner of an abandoned car park that overlooks the valley leading into the Third Ring. We are breathless, sweating and fatigued from the trauma of the previous days, but Aurora has assured me that a path forward will be available by nightfall. Cool waves emanate from her as she stands proudly on the edge of the parkade, hair blowing in the breeze. I strain to shield my eyes from the Rising Sun; in that moment, I feel the bond—the unspoken code between us—being rewritten. We are slowly moving away from one another, though I understand neither the rhyme nor the reason as to why it is happening. Perhaps she can see something I should also be able to see, but my time in Level Z has damaged my ability to unite with her thoughts. She steps off the edge and sits next to me, eyeing the remnants of blood under her fingernails. I yearn to touch her, but I know that time has passed forever as we inch closer to the End. Soon we will be ghosts traversing the open spaces of the inner rings.

"We'll wait here until nightfall. By then, our way out should make itself known near the cusp of the valley," she says softly.

We lay our heads down as the day grows brighter and warmer, the axe of fate drawing closer to our throats.

ONE NIGHT BRIDGE*

o   o   o   o

Night descends, playfully petting our skin. We make our way toward the mouth of the valley, breathing gently while keeping to the shadows. I see a purple glow on the horizon; hidden among the trees is a neon lit bridge, spanning the divide between the Third and Fourth Rings. My head aches as shifting memories of Leon's death reverberate through my skull. Now, as Aurora and I stand on the precipice of the Third Ring with a trail of blood behind us, very little makes sense—though, has it ever? Aurora, Leon... It all feels fabricated on some level, just like I feel fabricated by an infernal machine at the heart of the galaxy.

Aurora turns to me.

"That's One Night Bridge. It appears randomly, and it's how most people get into the Third Ring without anyone noticing. We'll be stuck here indefinitely if we don't go now."

"It appears randomly? Then this is what you saw! You know how this all ends."

Her dilated eye fills with a tear before she gently wipes it away. She turns her attention back to the bridge, glowing and pulsing with a dreamy spectral light. *How can something like this exist?* I think.

"It just does," Aurora rasps.

"How are you in my head, Aurora?" I ask, a quiver in my voice.

"I've always been there; you should know that by now. Let's go."

Aurora moves swiftly through the vegetation. As we near the

bridge, a low vibration seizes our chests. It's powerful, soothing. At its threshold, we are bathed in a deep fluorescence; the entire structure is translucent, yet it suspends a deep purple light—as if by magic. Sensing that I am being choked by fear and doubt, she extends her hand to me as we take our first steps onto the bridge.

"Do you feel that warmth?" I mutter, barely able to speak.

She nods, looking pensively over her shoulder to see if we are being followed. The bridge into the Third Ring leads us to a canopy of trees just above an old settlement. If I look hard enough, I know I will be able to see the remains of my missing friends. Skeletons of bodies, skeletons of memories... Both amount to the same thing in the end: bleached bones with no flesh to animate them.

Leaving the comfort of the woods, the air becomes acrid and thick. We descend into the settlement. I try not to think too deeply; I am positive that my thoughts are no longer mine—they belong to the woman in front of me, and I am no longer certain she is real.

EVERYWHERE AT THE END OF TIME*

○ ○ ○ ○

The settlement—many homes abandoned, uninhabitable, or completely destroyed by the progression of time—sits enshrouded in a dense chemical mist that burns my eyes as we walk with caution through the streets. The few people who come outside look at us like we are apparitions. Aurora stays close to my side as we pass through a town square at the heart of the Ring. She is in my head, speaking in soft tones.

"...Can you hear me? Don't speak out loud. The people who live here are afraid of outsiders. Our presence has been a big disturbance to them—you probably noticed. Stay near me, don't act rashly, and we'll find our way to our destination soon enough, okay? Nod if you understand."

I nod, thrusting my hands deep into my pockets while keeping my eyes down, the locals scrutinizing us with their gaze, their desiccated faces infiltrating our thoughts. Aurora's voice rings through my mind once more as we turn off the main road into a series of narrow side streets with blacked-out windows.

"Don't let their eyes meet yours, that's the most dangerous thing you can do; they have become paranoid because of their exposure to this mist. If someone approaches, turn away quickly. Follow my lead until we get to where we need to be, which isn't too far—if I remember correctly. Understand?"

Nodding again, we continue through the narrow streets until we come upon an isolated grouping of interconnected buildings.

At the end of the row, we are greeted by a large door spray painted with the words *Die Tür Ist Zu.* I stare at the familiar words, but their context has been lost. I shudder. The teetering feeling of a mind unfurling stalls our movements. Aurora's voice melds with a thousand others, coagulating in the centre of my head.

"*What's wrong? Get a hold of yourself, you're slipping away. We need to get inside, but we can't if you're strangling our movements with whatever it is that's eating at you... Let it go so we can move inside.*"

The moment the thought is complete, the door swings open as though guided by a gentle breeze, both stunning us and instantly increasing our paranoia. We are greeted by the heavy smell of pirated tobacco. A tiny, moving glow illuminates the depths of the antechamber. Looming before us, splitting in half, two bodies lurch out of the darkness like spectral gods overwriting the substance of their creation. Though they now have smooth feminine features, long eyelashes, and glistening lips—and they wear matching leather pants and tight jackets—I know them by intuition: the Twins, meeting me for the third time. One of them speaks.

"Hello again. It took you a long time to reach us through this madness. Step inside."

THE TRANSFORMATION*

o   o   o   o

Their large machetes glisten in the industrial glow of the building's antiquated lighting; they twist the handles in their hands, desiring a kill or, at the very least, blood. Leon... I have to pay for Leon. I know I have brought them here, conjured from the cauldron of a thousand suppressed thoughts. Aurora stands unblinkingly by my side, flashing an occasional smile in their direction.

The three of them look at each other curiously, sizing each other up, before one of the Twins motions us toward a staircase. I feel a tingling in my head.

"Do whatever they say, no matter how extreme or violent... This is all predestined, even if it goes against your reason. Nod if you understand; I know you can't think straight anymore."

She is correct. I can't think straight. Time stretches to infinity as we climb the stairs, and I have unfailing belief in her words: she has absolute faith from a leper who fell for a goddess. On the second floor, a series of fluorescent lights reveal a large space filled with stainless steel tables, immersive baths, surgical instruments, and an assortment of knives and chemicals. The smell is clean without being antiseptic, unlike similar rooms I have been in. We are handcuffed to one another while the Twins ready the room. They unsheath large hooks and cutting tools and turn on equipment that drones low and steady; the atmosphere reeks of death. Aurora remains motionless, but there is an unmistakable twinkle in her Ziggy eye. I look at her lovingly, sensing a sadness behind the visage that I have adored since the beginning.

One of the Twins speaks. "Now we're going to prepare your friend."

They unfasten Aurora's cuffs, leaving me attached to a nearby pipe. I sit helplessly while she is rough-handled. I watch them slap her face and lick her exposed flesh, then seethe with anger as the clothing is cut from her body, her exposed flesh glistening in the cold luminescence. They shave her head as well as the rest of the hair on her body: legs, arms, eyebrows—even the tiny triangle above her vagina. The hair is swept aside into piles of insignificant matter. Her gaze never wavers from mine, instructing me to shut my eyes and open my mind.

"Your fear is rising, I can tell. Don't lose your resolve now, not at the critical moment! This is almost over, but there is something you will have to do. Do not question it."

They strap Aurora to a table. One Twin pulls a gold-plated gun from his pocket and places it against the back of my head before unfastening my cuffs. The kiss of the barrel propels me towards Aurora's naked body, where I am handed a length of rope by the second Twin.

"The transformation is nearly complete. You have to finish it before the final exchange can be made, or you'll go to your graves together. Your choice."

Her eyes tell me everything. The eyes... Always the eyes.

Integrated Capstone Event

∘　∘　∘　∘

Timestretch. The moment feels like hours as I look at Aurora more deeply than I ever have before, my soul vibrating in union with hers, not wanting to move or initiate the inevitable, but the length of rope is already in my hand, its purpose known. One casualty, one life that feels like a million screaming at me from every direction—her gaze pleading with me to end it all with force and a ring of fibre. I can no longer stand the look on her face, so I close my eyes, wrapping the rope tenderly around her neck. The Twins chuckle to themselves. She gurgles and gasps for breath as I pull the two ends of the rope in opposite directions across her throat, but I don't dare look, imagining instead all the vaporous moments we had together that culminated in bodily bliss while wiping our minds of the present. The Twins urge me to pull harder, to feel her last warm breath brush my cheek. I feel a profound, rage-wrapped guilt telling me to die with Aurora. Then, the death rattle. The Twins roar with laughter. My mind goes silent as I drop to my knees and release the rope that ended Aurora. I reach for her cheek and weep, the Twins' incessant laughter fading into the background. I have never known the sting of such tears. To see the brightest flame of love and obsession fade so quickly... Her hand slips off the table and hangs there like a branch stripped of its leaves. The image of her lifeless body sears itself into the stone wall of my mind's eye, though I immediately want it washed away forever. My breath lost, the Twins nowhere to be found, I collapse on the ground next to Aurora's fresh corpse, paralyzed by the impact of what I have done.

Then, Aurora's words in my mind once more: *"There is something more you will have to do. There is work to be done."*

PART THREE

NEW FLESH

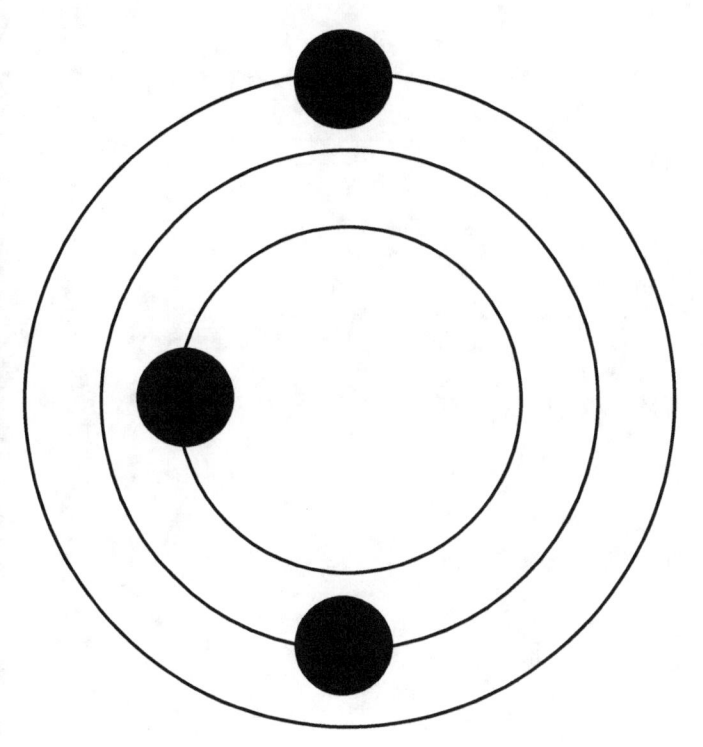

SECRECY/BODY POSTURE

○   ○   ○

What disappears becomes troublesome. Emerald green hair a moment ago; my past is all black bile, ass, and mouth. Too many times I've sat in front of the silver mirror (1995–2000)—I cross the terminal zone like passing over Daath... Chaos. Abyss. *Let me die at the end among the cherry blossoms, stars in a pool of my blood.* Inhaling the alien dust, I'm the body dancing outside myself. Invisible barriers in the obscure winter depths, listening, dying over and over. *The seasons come full circle, and as winter descends, a stranger brings the warmth that is a clarion call to my laughter*.* Hazel eyes. Walls. The comedown into A.'s moans above my astral quivering flesh. Flesh melting, *yes*, melting into a river that is liquid flesh... My tongue darts in and out of the ballrooms, tasting her lady cum, dreaming of ice. No better taste. Nothing compares. Her reflection bleeds eternally in me, just like the rest of her. There must be a solution, a way out, a way forward. She is of a nomadic people—cut off from the rest, but dead just the same. Unchangeable. *A surgeon, a cadaver, and a resurrection. Gentle violence—the lingering sting becomes the balm for the broken bits. Piecemeal reconstruction in fading hues of violet*.* Every wall, every mirror is rigged—remember that. Remember everything. There she embalms herself, mummifies herself, names herself—falling inevitably into a tomb of her own making.

Undressing of A. Strip poker without the cards. Dead on the table. I study every fold of her body. Hand between legs revealing the black nail polish adorning her fingers. Chant: *The Universe is an* *ocean of dazzling light, and on it dance the waves of life and death*. Lust is the quest of the flesh for the Unknown*.* The heat and light from her eyes have become icicles of tears, frozen in perpetual sadness. I turn away from her and laugh like THEY did. She has become a barely visible stem, an almost imperceptible cold prop, caught in ice, frost, glass, and gel. Let the embalmed body of A. congeal.

TRANSITORY MAN AND HIS DWELLINGS*

o o o

Cleansing of the body. Hers and mine. With rigor mortis setting in, I rinse myself carefully in one of the immersive baths, sensing the centres of sin that I want to cut from myself but can't: heart, brain, fingers, eyes. I move Aurora's corpse into a cool, aromatic pool, where I wash the coagulated blood from her skin. *Dead in the morning and born at night, so man goes on forever, unenduring as the foam on the water*.* Her green hair floats in the lavender scented pool while her breasts, now slightly discoloured, rise over the gentle ripples, nipples pointing heavenward.

I stand over her, naked, and stare at the dark ring around her neck where I had held the rope so tightly. *How was I able to commit such an act?* I ask myself over and over. She looks peaceful, just as I've heard the dead often do—pulled from the senseless vacuum of life into a new stream about which we can only speculate. Draining the pool, I plug in a large space heater and place it by her cleansed flesh. Every action I make feels predestined, just like she said, spurring me on to complete a task that becomes more obvious as time slips by. While her body dries, I fill an empty pool with bags of coarse salt, spreading it evenly over the bottom to create a nest for her. I pack more salt around the slight curves and on top of the quickly fading sheen of her flesh. *Nobody likes having salt rubbed into their wounds, even if it's the salt of the earth*.* I sit on my haunches for hours, drifting in and out of consciousness, tripping over old memories, real and imaginary, occasionally touching Aurora's leg or arm to see how dry it has become. I weep. I laugh like a maniac. I scream at the top of my lungs and curse the fuck out of the Twins, wherever they disappeared to. A large bay window covered with a sheet catches my attention while I wipe tears from my face. Standing, I look outside and see that night has fallen again. The streets of the Third Ring are empty. I return to Aurora's corpse, kneading the cool, dead skin under my palm.

OSTARA

o o o

Aurora's corpse remains packed in salt for four days while I rest on an old sofa in an exterior room. Physical pains. Mental strain. Waking suddenly from a deep sleep to find that I am alone. I sometimes stumble into the room where she rests and flick on the light. Staring at the salted mound, I desperately attempt to forget how I have reached this point in time, then I go back to the couch and throw a thin blanket over my body, shutting my eyes tight until I fall back asleep. The painted pictures in my mind—for I cannot call the images I see in my mind "dreams"—feel like manifestations of the madness I experienced in the Chamber; they are hallucinatory mosaics of past lives never lived and repressed nightmares. On the morning of the fifth day, my hand dips into the salt and lifts her pale head. Brushing small particles from her brow, I eye her quizzically, as though I have discovered an ancient object at the bottom of the sea.

Let the waters bring forth abundantly the moving creature that hath life, and fowl that may fly above the earth in the open firmament of heaven*. The suppleness of her frame and flesh has lost its beauty and become a heap of rigid bones, soon to be broken by my hand. The intense, claustrophobic space of my dreams pushes me to complete the task she has subliminally sent to the centre of my being. This is only the first step—the room, my City of Ur—the tables and baths... The landscape where the bird is to be plucked and dissected before resuming flight. Aurora tasked me with giving her wings, but I had to destroy her to fulfill her personal prophecy;

it is a prophecy that I have not yet begun to understand. I let instinct guide me as I remove her from the salt and ease her into a bath of honey and cinnamon, where she remains immersed for four more days.

My energy begins to ebb.

Wayfaring Stranger in the Bardo
○ ○ ○

"Can you hear me? Can you see me? Look to the end of the hall."

She speaks to me as I dream; I see a vague outline of her body in the distance, waiting for me. We stand in a passageway floating over an azure pool that stretches to infinity. I strain my eyes as I walk toward her shape, but as I approach, she appears to recede. I feel strangely comfortable here, as though all the chains of the present have been lifted off. Gravity seemed to have inverted, and I have no sense of time; it has flown off in all directions.

"You still haven't answered my questions." Her voice has changed —it sounds younger, softer. It frightens me, and I think it can't be her, but I answer. "Yes, I can hear you perfectly, but I can only see a small portion of you. You're too blurry, like static." A row of wavy teeth appear through a smile, the water below us growing darker. I am confused. I can't see a source of light diminishing to change its colour. The passageway grows smaller as I stand there, frozen and mute. "You look different now. This is not how I remember you. What have you done to yourself?" When was the last time I looked in a mirror, I wonder.

Aurora has likely seen my face more times than I have seen it myself... I begin to panic, searching the narrow passage for something to catch my reflection, but everything I touch melts before me. "Go to my body and look at my face again. That is who you truly are." My body shakes—or what I deemed to be my body—as Aurora fades from sight, the passageway rapidly dimming and narrowing. The floor begins to collapse into the water, which has now turned jet-black. I am dropped into its depths; it feels like thick syrup, clogging my pores, suffocating me.

When I open my eyes, the first solar rays are passing through the holes in the old curtain, warming my cheeks. I touch my face lightly, uncertain if it belongs to me.

ENGINE OF THE MIND

○ ○ ○

I n the absence of faith—Aurora had been my only faith in life—I set to task on her rigid corpse, its brightness long extinguished, ready to peer inside for the first time. I stand over her without emotion or tremble and attempt to see my true self in her dead skin.

In her, I look at what I have lost—the dense Saturn lead weighs on my chest where her memory rests. Her body glistens with an amber sheen as I raise her from the pool. Rinsing the honey and cinnamon solution from her corpse gives me time to explore the familiar areas. I recall caressing them with my fingers. "Don't linger too long," I say to myself. "It will only bring you pain." Palming a scalpel, I make an incision from ear to ear across her hairline, then peel the skin off the back of her skull. Aurora must have had ultimate foresight: a Gigli saw sits on the table, waiting to cut through her dura matter. Once I understand the logistics of the saw, the top of her skull comes off easily, and I pause to marvel at her brain, which still seems to pulsate instructions to me from its atrophied state. Placing my hands around the soft lobes, I lift the grey matter from its burrow of bone and examine it from every angle. Her face retains an aura of peace although I have desecrated her body, the summation of my passions and desires gone cold with her passing by through the wall of death. Lifting her brain in my hands, I hold it over a tank I have filled with acid. I give it a light kiss and feel the smooth grooves of her occipital lobe upon my lips before I drop it in and watch it bubble into nothingness. I am overcome with a surge of energy as the days and nights slowly evaporate into the past. I resubmerge what remains of her corpse in the honey and cinnamon and watch as the thick liquid fills the cavity where the great machine of her mind once laid.

CLOTHED IN THE SKIN OF THE DEAD

o o o

I mmersed in the shallow puddle of my mindmelt after days without solid rest, I feel an awkward, subtle shift toward a vacant, claustrophobic space within me. Though not without harm, I have managed to make it back from the narrow, airless room of my thoughts, traversing the unforgiving waters of my consciousness while sticking my third eye on a metaphorical pin. Perhaps it is the weight of trauma pushing against that thin line of sanity, but I know better. I have always inhabited the dry territory of time; it drifts and shifts according to its own whims, inevitably guiding me to, once again, remove Aurora from her honeyed tomb.

By this point, Aurora's flesh has taken on a deep grey hue. I bathe her with utmost care, even though I know she has long since stopped feeling anything at all. I have a selection of knives at my disposal; they have been neatly stored on the wall, and I turn each one over in my hand to check the sharpness, often glimpsing my sallow reflection in the carbon grooves.

I make the first deep cut. It runs from the base of her throat through the pillow of flesh where I used to lay my head and terminates in the soft hill of her pubis; here I had often placed soft kisses or bites, depending on the heat of my blood. I trace deep marks into the flesh with a surgical precision that I was unaware I possessed, peeling layers of skin away from muscles that appear taut and strong, even in death. My steadiness falters as I gaze at her, the remainder of her corpse flayed beyond recognition. *I wish her eyes would open.* One does not always need depth of courage to complete a difficult task; one only needs the will to complete it. With a surge of unfailing strength, I slice the remaining skin from her face and hold it across the palms of my hands before I lay it in a mound with all the rest. Days and nights pass; I gradually dismember what is left of her body, then watch my memories dissolve in a vat of acid.

I keep a few parts, praying to St. Bartholomew for forgiveness.

Opening the Mouth

o   o   o

Peseshkaf—also a serpent-headed blade, consecrated in her blood... It hovers over her severed head, rocking back and forth between my index finger and thumb like a pendulum. She needs food and water to slake her thirst and fill her belly in the afterlife, but I cannot provide them. "She is cleansed of me," I think. Cleansed of my past and my filth. *"Let me hear joy and gladness; let the bones you have crushed rejoice."** The pools are drained, and the tools and instruments are put to rest. My work is complete. The last bit of stability abandons my hands as soon as I realize most of her body has been dissolved to nothing; I smile like a fool who has finally outdone himself without much effort. I find an electric razor and shave my body to remove what little I can of myself—for her. I speak the words: *"My mouth is opened by (....), my mouth's bonds are loosed by my (....-...). (.....) the Magician has come fully equipped with the spells (...-....)—he looses the bonds of (....) from my mouth—(....) has given me my hands."** Bowing to the floor, I pray to Pasithea and Hypnos, the goddesses who have always guided my life—or, at least, I believe they follow close behind me, whispering in my ears as I attempt to shake away the remnants of a life that never felt like it truly belonged to me. Laughter again. The silence of the building pierces me. I am out of tears, and my abdomen hurts; nothing more can be drawn from me in this moment. Even in death, even as the guts of the material world have loosened their grip on me and Aurora, the dripping mouth of a hidden Demiurge spits me back out into the burgeoning eschaton.

THE SKULL

○　○　○

I lay naked and prone in the cool building where the hinges creak, staring at a yellowish glow that falls upon Aurora's skull. I am the dutiful *kapalika*, the one who cleaned and bleached the bone, imagining her delicate features as they fade into the recesses of my mind. There is no cure for me, no absolution. Aurora was the great liberator of my spirit, and I am the parasitic wasp who dismantled her piece by lovely piece. *"Repulsiveness of the hacked and scattered, repulsiveness of the hacked and scattered."** I recall small electrodes being placed on my temples—when, exactly, I cannot say—the antiquated method resetting the tired neurons while language flowed from my lips, scarring everyone forever.

I can only surmise which memories evaporated as the electrical pulses whipped around my brain, nevermind the damage caused by the man-made poisons that were pumped into my bloodstream. My skin pressed into the cold tile, I feel a vast emptiness. The process is complete—a double death, so to speak: one of the flesh, one of the spirit. My own time feels short; it trickles out like water from a broken bucket. Taking Aurora's skull into the adjacent room where I have unsuccessfully attempted to sleep for countless nights, I hold it close to my chest before wrapping myself in a thin blanket. The final gleamings of the day filter through the tattered curtain. After a deep breath, I exhale slowly until the last bit of air exits my lungs. I close my eyes, turn on my side, and hug the skull close to my body. *"Till I take vaster attitudes / and strut upon my stem / disdaining men, and oxygen / for arrogance of them."** (Emily Dickinson)

THE MIRROR

o o o

Where do I lie now? Or, did I ever lie down at all? *"I'm a fading spectre in a room layered with yesterdays, a prisoner of a haunted past."** I am a ball of silver, twisting and morphing. Swallowing it all, part and parcel, tooth, hand, and eye. *"Que haya suenos es raro, que haya espejos. Que el usual y gastado repertorio de cada dia incluya el ilusorio, orbe profundo que urden los reflejos."** Where do I go now? Out through the mouth or through the slippery esophagus and into time's reeking intestines? I never dared to look into a fucking mirror to see my tired face melt away. Reflect no image, reflect no thought back on myself. Maybe I have given up the imaginary... Something seeks to pull me apart at the seams, drawn and quartered. I can no longer tell which direction I am travelling. Perhaps in circles to the centre: duplicating, replicating, dividing, dwindling, bubbling, descending into the lowest areas where the Hand reaches or the penis penetrates. Nothing touches me here, in the vast fields of that other place, where I hide on the opposite side of the glass, barely moving—if movement is even possible. Aurora would know to look for me here, in this vast liminal space, if she ever knew me. Can she hear my voice, just like I used to hear hers across the desert of my thoughts? All credit to her: *"The antiseptic wash has sterilized the pinks, yellows, and blues of memory. We have razed the forests of jewels glistening in the penumbra of halogen bulbs."** Where did we lose each other? I try to laugh, but nothing. I hold my mouth open, attempt to catch the past on my tongue. She can no longer see me; I can no longer see myself, though I still speak. Galaxy spiralling, spreading the cosmic dust, hurtling toward the black hole of time... *Mirror upon mirror. Reflections of an infinite emptiness held by a vacant gaze. The search for a non-existent self is a spiral into the abyss.** Her words echo, and I echo along with her.

The Anal Staircase*

○ ○ ○

Muffled sounds reach my ears through the icy pool of water I've been lying in for what feels like a lifetime, adrift in the comfort of sleep. A tube allows me to breathe easily while my body rejuvenates in the healing waters; my mind is calm and comforted. Rising from the shallow pool, I shake the water from my emerald locks, and turn on the large space heater. The room is just as I remember it: sparse, clean, bright—a perfect environment for someone like me who demands a certain level of silence and peace. I stand before the mirror, running my hands over my breasts, hips, and pubis before mounting the strap-on to my body. I tie my hair into a high bun, dressing in a kimono patterned with chrysanthemums.

The adjoining rooms in this complex—the only space in the Third Ring not swimming with fetid, disgusting humans—are my refuge. Here, in this space that is so close to the Centre, all the pliant energy climbs over the walls and dissipates back to the Fifth Ring. Sauntering down the bright orange hallway, I come to my favourite door: it conceals the Twins. Blindfolded, they groan when I enter. My heavy barefoot steps have roused them, but gagged with lead balls, they cannot speak. Fugitive Twins—identical, lean—taken in the heart of the Third Ring by me and my Sisters immediately following the death of their friend and leader, L. I'm not often prone to violence, but I made short work of him before I dismembered his corpse and left it in an outer district, hoping for the night creatures to tear at it with their dirty teeth.

My hands wrap perfectly around their smooth throats—they've

probably lost all sense of time after so many days spent at my mercy. Their asses bleed from all the punishment, blood caked to hairless thighs. I remove the lead ball gags so they can speak, but I leave them blindfolded so my intentions remain a mystery. Placing the balls in my pocket, I call the Sisters to assist me. They appear softly as ghosts.

"Prop them up facing the wall and prepare the rods in the fire."

One of the Twins begins to shake violently, perhaps hoping that his spasms will prevent the coming onslaught of pain, but the other one knows better; he has accepted that any reaction will lead to more agony. He's learning, the other is beyond stubborn. One of my Sisters, dressed in a hooded satin gown, grabs his neck roughly and spits in his face.

"Stop fucking moving, or I'll slit your goddamn throat."

I smile. He stills after my Sister slaps his face. She raises him to his feet by a pulley, his wrists raw. His twin moans and whimpers, and I kick him firmly in the ribs. I position myself behind the suspended brother and inch a large strap-on into his gaping ass, digging my nails into his neck. My Sisters watch in rapt ecstasy as I thrust my hips into him repeatedly.

"Bring me a rod," I say gently.

Grinning as I pull out, I slide one of the rods into his wide-open asshole.

My hand smothers his screams.

The Dancer Stripped of Her Skin

o o o

My Sisters—in mind if not in flesh—guide me down to the main level of the building, then open the heavy gate that leads into my personal paradise. I stand beneath a large bay window that overlooks the Third Ring; it is from here that I often observe the infinitely unsettled collective, dead from the inside out, fluttering about. Time moves in all directions this close to the Centre, tearing me away from old perceptions of myself. My dreams and nightmares take me to the height of ecstasy.

The Twins do their penance with bleeding asses.

The Sisters run warm water into the limestone pool, creating a fresh womb for my gestation. I imagine myself as a neolithic rock, jagged and sharp—a challenging object for the hands of the saintly ones. The Sisters and I found each other by a strong attraction of foreign energy pulsing from the Centre. It draws all types of transient beings into our path, ready to join us or perish. Sinking into the healing elemental water, I think about my death and the demise of others. The path will eventually end, but I still have far to travel.

Their lithe bodies slide into the pool. Soft brushes in their hands move roughly across my skin, flaking it away. My body relaxes under their scrubbing, and I feel the heat of their breath inch closer. Their lips touch my collarbone. I become softer with each planted kiss, each movement of the brush; I am the perfect sphere, weathered and shaped by the mouths of obedient equals.

Rainbow Obsidian Key

○   ○   ○

Night. Perpetual night. The cloak I always wear, even when touched by the pulse of the solar disk. The Third Ring buzzes with the sounds of dealers, holy men, and a million other strange beings. The night is alive with those who forego sleep to dream while awake, and the evening brims with hypnotic noise as I seek The Collector. He is certain to have what I need. The Sisters leave me when I feel the need to venture out like this, confident that I'll return unscathed. In the bazaar, far removed from all the ordinary sellers, the landscape opens to me, even as the choking, claustrophobic air descends. I make my way to the cellar, where The Collector lives. Only a few keys to his dwelling exist, all carved from rainbow obsidian.

Moving down the smooth stone steps, the cacophony of the bazaar fades. The limestone path to his Chamber is a liminal space of dense calm, sparsely lit—just like I imagine the Bridge of Sighs in the floating city. My key slips easily into the hole... When the door opens, I find him sitting in the corner of the room, pouring himself a glass of a golden liquid. He turns slightly.

"Back so soon? I figured it would be at least a couple weeks before you reappeared. You look different."

"That's what everyone says. I snagged L. and his boys. He's dead, and the Twins are hanging out to dry," I laugh.

The Collector snickers and motions for me to sit at a table. He taps a finger to his lips, looking contemplative while leaning back in his chair.

"Have you ever had a daydream where you feel that another

version of yourself has already played out a situation, like a wave of déjà-vu?"

"That feeling seems to linger around me lately, now that you mention it... ever since I came out of the pool from my regenerative sleep, in fact. I'm here because I need more dream powder."

He takes a sip of his drink before responding.

"There's a problem. The raw materials for the powder can only be found closer to the Centre. I'll have to make a journey beyond the Third Ring. You can either come along, or you can wait for me to return. But even at the best of times, the latter can be a poor choice: the Second Ring is often dubbed a point of no return."

"If that's the case, how have you been so fortunate thus far?"

"The weight of my karma must be light... Or I'm just that lucky."

I inhale deeply and exhale slowly, contemplating my decision. "I'll need a couple days to prepare. Don't leave without me."

THE PUPPETS*

o   o   o

The Twins were perfectly prepared during my excursion. My Sisters have turned them into literal objects of high art: their appendages (heads included) are tautly stretched and strapped to a series of ropes; it will be easy to manipulate every movement like the reticulated wings of a moth. For the first time since their capture, their blindfolds have been removed. The Sisters tell me they writhed and screamed as light flooded their synapses, having been immersed in darkness for over a month. Where did the time go?

Staring lovingly at their naked, bruised, and bloodied bodies suspended above me, a rising tide of erotic energy ascends to the centre of my head.

*"I am like a puppet sitting here. It's not just I. All of us are puppets. Nature is pulling the strings, but we believe that we're acting."** The depth of fear on their faces is palpable, making the sensation even more intense—so much so that I feel it pulse in my forehead and behind my eyes. Pulling one of the ropes thrusts their heads back, exposing the white skin of their masculine throats. I watch their apples rise and fall as they gasp for air. Do they know what awaits them? A soft end to a period of pain, the conclusion of a cycle that began with the splitting of cells inside the womb. I pull another rope, and their arms are brought behind their backs, deepening the strain that eats at them like a thousand maggots burrowing into a suitable host.

I hold out my hand, my eyes still fixed on them: my body reaches the ideal vibration as one of the Sisters passes me a hunting knife. The other brings over a golden urn and places it beneath the first Twin, who, surprisingly, is now as quiet as his brother. The Twins open their eyes for a second before clenching them shut. In unison, the Sisters begin the death hum.

I raise my hand to the throat of the first Twin, deftly open the carotid artery, then watch the crimson waterfall fill the blessed urn.

THE STATE OF THE BLOOD AFTER DEATH

o o o

B y degrees, the blood begins to clot from the open wounds inflicted upon the bodies. The corpses hang like withered branches in the sultry light while the Sisters dilute the blood that accumulated in the urn. *"Death holds up an all-seeing mirror, the mirror of past actions."** L. got off easy with only a bolt of lead to finish his earthly cycle, allowing me to save my energies for what I had just accomplished: creating a bridge between ecstatic life and horrific death, the great dynamic that seems to exist in any world, including the Third Ring—the one point in the triangle that manifests anything of worth. Not one to succumb to faith, I rely on my own strength and the strength of my Sisters. *"Some kinds of sister-love are stronger than blood."** We are prepared to leave the corpses behind; I fulfilled my purpose through their subtle manipulations. The warehouse, the Chamber... Everything else is now meaningless. The real goal—the endpoint—lies beyond those bodies, across the threshold between the Third and Second Ring.

The Sisters seal the urn and prepare it for transport, sensing that I will soon lay claim to the power within the vital fluid. I wrap myself in purple satin, dip my fingers into the urn, and press the blood to my lips. I replay the scene in my mind—perhaps even watching it unfold on another plane in another time—remembering every nuance of movement as I savour the metallic rose bouquet of those young men on my tongue.

The citizens of the Ring barely take notice of us as we move quickly through the narrow passages and side streets, a colourful blur against a drab background, stopping occasionally to wet our lips with the urn nectar or the lips of one another, the rattle of obscene death slipping further into the background, causing me to momentarily forget that I had felt the rush of blood through my veins.

THE PEAK

o   o   o

As time slows, my pulse, heartbeat, and thoughts slow with it. The Sisters and I have reached The Collector's door. In my absence, he has readied himself for a discreet edging toward the boundary of the Third Ring. In the short time since I've last seen him—how much time, I can't really tell—his face has changed. He has softer features, brighter eyes... At first, I believe I am imagining his transformation, but when he speaks, his voice has the clear crispness of someone half his age.

"Have you brought any weapons?" he asks.

We nod. Our means of protection are rudimentary but effective; we carry several large hammers, a bo staff, canisters of mace, and the meat cleaver I used to dissect the body of L. after I killed him. A bullet had not been enough; the splendid virgin steel of the cleaver settled any remaining adverse feelings I had toward him.

"It will take us at least a day and a half to make it to the Impasse Region, where our chance of death increases exponentially. Don't bother to ask questions—what matters is your state of mind. As one wends their way through the region, the path inevitably changes. Logically, this may change the disposition of the individual as well."

I look at him through narrowed lids, wondering how he has managed to be so slippery in his appearance—a quality I thought only I possessed.

L. befriended me and led me to believe that we shared a connection; he proved to be the chaotic principle in the nether space of my thoughts. I began to believe my existence was for some higher purpose. Too much dream powder... Or maybe not enough. Regardless, it will all be settled soon. At least, this is what I think as we set out together, the sun at its zenith and the rising moon to come.

Flanked by the Sisters, The Collector blazes a trail. Within a couple of hours, the land flattens, and the settlements and buildings become more sparse. As the day progresses and the Sun begins its descent into the horizon, wolves appear in the distance.

The Collector pauses to light a wooden torch and pass us each a capsule of dream powder.

"Take it. We'll be walking through the night; the powder will help us see. We should reach the Impasse Region as dawn approaches. The wolves are out. They'll either guide us to our destination or eat us. Hard to fucking predict."

We consume the capsules. I'm flooded with a familiar sensation, one that I have nearly forgotten due to my time underwater. As my perception changes vibration, I can think only of L., kneeling in front of me, his hands tied behind his back, asking to whisper something in my ear. His face contorted, his breath in my ear...

"I've seen you so many times, Aurora, in the shadow of the Obelisk..."

FULL MOON MOTH

o o o

We rest by a hill, the subtle glow of The Collector's torch burning freely, the wolves baying and shifting on the periphery of our vision, keeping us under watch. I feel the dream powder begin to sift through my arms, legs, and eyes as the Sisters lean into my body, unaccustomed to the powder's effects. Their warm breath on my neck heightens my pleasure for a moment, just as it did when we all bathed in the limestone pool; I remember we're carrying an urn of blood. I stand and face my companions, positioning my head upwards, toward the moon blazing in full brilliance. *Sphinx ligustri* in the sky? *"The moth enters the heart ... the pathway to yourself is through your resistances."** The Sisters stand beside me, their drugged faces heavy with perspiration; they breathe heavily on my neck. A light sweat forms on my brow, even though the night air is cool and refreshing. Their combined breath becomes kisses, awakening me to the true nature of the moment. My head begins to spin away. Flash of the torch, laughter from The Collector's mouth... The Sisters press their fingers against my breasts... I'm lost now. My naked flesh shines in the lunar glow as the tiny moths dance. I lie on the hardened earth as they pour tiny rivulets of blood from the urn over my skin. They crouch over me; I smile. They smile too, but their lips morph and shift as the powder settles ever deeper into our minds. *"Memory creates a hallucination of the past, desire creates a hallucination of the future."** I laugh with my eyes closed and feel the last bit of blood being licked off my body. Silence. In that one solid moment, I feel whole again, before the entirety of my being collapses from the weight of the stars and moon above me.

The Collector then stands over us, his glowing torch a radiant kaleidoscope of colour, and motions for us to move on, back into the belly of the night.

SOLAR SHIP VOYAGE

o   o   o

We must be heading East, for as the hours wear on and our visions and ecstasies begin to wane, the Sun appears on the horizon, shocking us back to life after a night of introspection, the wolves baying a symphony in the distance. The Collector has been oddly silent for most of the trek, making the Sisters and I suspicious of what we will encounter once we reach the edge of the Third Ring. We enter the Impasse Region, and The Collector turns to us.

He says that only I can go forward; the Sisters will remain behind. They quickly become a distant blur.

I take a lead ball from my pocket and turn it in my hand.

"What do you have there, Aurora?"

"My means of escape."

He smirks and looks directly at the rising Sun, its powerful heat beaming intensely on our skin. Then he stops, adamant that we rest. He says there is much we need to do and discuss before we can continue.

"In order to be granted access into the Second Ring, the border crossing requires that the candidate perform a passage ritual in the Hall of Serpents. I recommend you take some dream powder and bring the urn. My own passage has different criteria."

I nod. The air is still, and it's getting hotter with each passing minute. I take what little water we have and drink deeply, splashing a few drops over my face. The Collector removes his cloak and passes me his remaining supply of dream powder. I place it on my tongue, then prepare for the inevitable surge and distortion that will accompany the border crossing. I wistfully recall a distant memory from my younger years: I would raise my hands to the sky and capture the Sun between them, thinking myself clever for outsmarting the solar furnace. Guided by memory, I do the same now, completing a cycle of union between my past and present, uniting the two spheres of the sky: Sun and Moon

"You appear to be ready. Let's continue to the crossing. I'll walk behind you; they already know me."

With each step, the energy of the morning glow pierces my forehead, the light nearly blinding me. The gatekeeper, a tall man holding a ledger and wearing an ibis mask, stands idly in front of a large brass scale. I remove the lead balls from my pocket, and he motions for me to place them on the scale; it comes into perfect balance. I set the urn of blood at his feet.

"Consider this blood the *real* weight of my karmic debt."

The gate to the Hall of Serpents opens, and I glide through on a rising wave of dream powder.

THE PASSWORD*

o   o   o

Entering by way of a limestone hallway, I pass through a vestibule and arrive at a stairwell that ascends steeply, the air heavy with a scent of northern lilies. I find **enjoyment in untroubled ease.**

Climbing the stairs slowly, **a cicada and a little dove laugh at me, saying: we make an effort, then fly towards an elm or sapwood tree.** Maybe it's all a vision, maybe it's just a terrible distortion of the space around me, but the stairs narrow, **and before we reach it, we can do no more than drop to the ground.** The higher I go, the more the walls shine—expanding space evermore. I wonder **what use it is for this creature to rise 90,000 feet, then make for the South.** At the top of the stairwell, my absent body grounds itself for a brief moment: **the mushroom of the morning does not know (what takes place between) the spring and autumn.**

Across a threshold, I see a large rotunda cross-sectioned by a shallow pit lined with brass. Here, **in the bare and barren North, there is a dark and vast ocean—the Pool of Heaven.** Within the pit, lying coiled, is a serpent who awaits my caress. From the edge of the pit, I observe it in its meditative state. It lifts its head, then speaks to me telepathically: **The Perfect ~~Man~~ has no thought of Self; the Spirit-like ~~Man~~, none of merit; the Sagely-minded ~~Man~~, none of fame...** The serpent remains focused on me as I look into its reptilian eyes, observing my obscured past as it's transmitted back to me. I remove my clothing and carefully pick my way into the pit. The serpent appears to be smiling: **When the Sun and Moon come forth, if**

the torches have not been extinguished, is it not difficult for them to give light?

Kneeling before the snake, it rises to meet my eyes. I place a gentle kiss on its head.

BRAZEN SERPENT

o   o   o

My fingers, in a multitude of colours, glide over the serpent while it moves gracefully over my naked body. **I shall sleep peacefully through the night, free from anger after having seen myself liberated from the mouth of death.** Where has the Sun gone? Have I already forgotten its presence? The snake stops moving, resting its head between my breasts. I hear it speak to me through the currents of my thoughts. It says: **The knowing Self is not born, it dies not; it sprang from nothing, nothing sprang from it. The Ancient is unborn, eternal, everlasting. ~~HE~~ is not killed, though the body is killed.** Its tongue darts in and out of its mouth in rhythm; I remember that this creature will shed its skin, and **after leaving its body, they who have killed the Self go to the worlds of the Asuras**—like I go willingly into the Second Ring. The snake has stretched itself across the length of my body; we rest together like lovers and merge. I close my eyes, remembering I will not sleep until the powder has exhausted itself, reeling in **the face of truth hidden by a golden disk.**

Rising slowly, I cradle the serpent in my arms like I would a child, carrying it to the threshold that leads into the wilds of an unfamiliar land where **the ~~Father~~ replied: I shall give thee unto Death.** I place the serpent at my feet and open the door. I clothe myself while the serpent watches closely, my body lost because I cannot feel it. He knows my intention and, ultimately, the power I have over him, and he knows that **of all causes for sorrows, there is none as great as the death of mind—the death of man's body being only next to it.** Radiant light floods the limestone vestibule as I open the door. The serpent is by my side as the path narrows to a carved passage **where the sun rises in the East and sets in the extreme West—the position of all things is determined by these two points.**

HER LIPS WERE WET WITH VENOM

o   o   o

Dazzling sprawl—amidst the flash and burn of a million lights, a deep hum resonates across the Ring.

Metallic pathways connect buildings high above, like in the fevered dream of Urbicande and the dim corners of the Fifth. Had I felt the Fifth's slow blade across my throat while I was submerged under the therapeutic waters of the Chamber? I look back at the door. Has it been swallowed, or has it been closed? The serpent, coiled at my feet, speaks a final time: **The ~~King~~ of Death has no awe of the golden emblems of rank you wear...**

I grasp it by the head and straighten its body before opening its mouth to expose its fangs. Pressing them into my wrist, the deep sting of a primal force explodes in my veins as the poison enters my bloodstream. Setting him at my feet, we move toward the electron cloud of light ahead of us. I can barely see.

Dream powder or poison? No distinction. The downward pull of negative force, stronger than gravity. I place my lips around the wound created by my lover's fangs and suck out the poison; it mixes with my saliva, and I fall to my knees. He looks at me with indifference before coiling up once again beside my body. I'm spent. I lie on my back, the world upside down, his tongue hissing near my ear.

The weight is lifting now, between my measured breaths, allowing me to unfurl myself beneath the night sky: absent moon, absent stars. Only a glare ahead of me, inverted and bright, gives me some peace as the world falls away once more.

PART FOUR

THE CULT OF AURORA

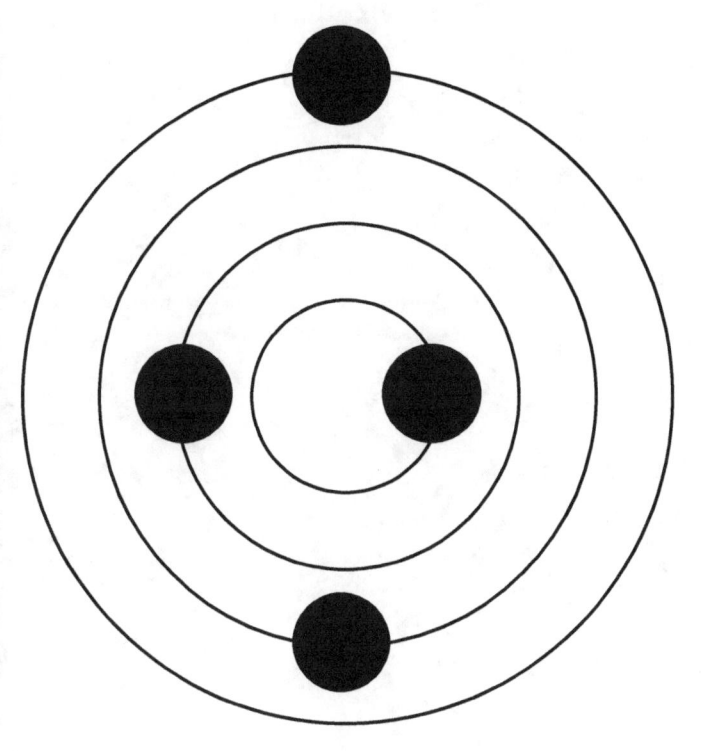

LI TOBLER AND THE CONJURATION
OF THE FOUR
o   o

I become inanimate—or at the very least porous, translucent. To the point where *They* can observe the pulsing of my organs and the flow of my blood. I dream of Li Tobler's suicide and Giger's awkward techno-cock penetrating my mind: his seed germinates in my pineal gland, then expands into the form of an elemental angel.

These names and images came from a spinning vortex, but they crouch on the fringes and stare at me vacantly. Perhaps I read about them somewhere.

I walk through the circular streets of the Second Ring. Beams of deep yellow light my face—it is a nameless but familiar sensation. I felt it when I passed through, its deep resonance running through my fingers and over my flesh to the very atoms of my being.

All the faces, the bodies that move slightly, that make a fast turn... They look at me from every direction and gaze upon my translucent flesh like I'm an alien creature. Maybe I am. Part of me wants to scream, which another part will not allow. "Stay silent," a voice—not my own—says inside me. Have I ever truly known my own voice? All this time... I must have forgotten.

Forgive me; tell me what to do.

Whatever you do, keep moving. We can be seen... *Us* in our entirety, or at the very least the physical part of our being. Their stares will entice you—they will lead to anxiety, obliteration. Beyond all these monstrous buildings and lights, deep in the core of the Ring, we will be safe from their gaze.

So, this is the *They*. Why do they have skin and we do not? Is this difference important?

No, it is not. They are human, certainly, but they favour the pleasures of physical embodiment and the bondage that keeps them enslaved to their flesh. Ignore them and keep moving.

I need to know where to go—the way forward, beyond this circle. People stare at me with expressions of frightened awe.

Move with stealth as we descend into the Ring.

I am not real, but even bereft of skin, I see, breathe, touch.

Keep walking. Descend the steps in front of you to the lowest point, then climb back up again, into the blinding neon.

I walk faster, past all the gawking faces, searching for a reflective surface. I want to see my grotesque visage. A set of stairs—just like the voice said—shifts down to a series of isolated bathing pools churning with mineral-green water. No one is around, at least for the moment, and I prepare to gaze at my reflection.

Are you certain you're brave enough to look? I'm not sure you are. We've been through a lot thus far, and what you see may shock you.

I'm going to open my eyes now. I want you to remain silent while I gather my thoughts. Wait... What do you mean by *we*?

Open our eyes, Aurora; you will see what has become of us since you entered this Ring. Our newest version of self has waded into the future, courtesy of the swelling of time.

I'm going to open them now. Slowly. I feel so cold, so aimless...

In this space, our head is encased in amber, preserved and

sustained by an unknown force.

My Left eye is permanently dilated, and the other looks sunken and sad. My hair is gone, my lips are cracked and peeled. Who—or what—am I?

We are the best of both worlds. We need to keep moving, descending until we disappear.

TUNE FROM THE MISSING CHANNEL

o o

S omething pursues us, Aurora. An entity of some
kind.

I hear you, but where are we?

Looking ahead, I see a small pocket of space along the descending path. It is wide enough for me to climb into and appears to be an old living space, abandoned but in good repair. A dusty television sits in the corner. A few other items lie scattered about.

This place feels familiar; it's like I've already inhabited this space.

Of course this place is familiar, Aurora. It's a permutation of all that came before: our wants, our dreams, our nightmares.

Why do you keep talking? Why do you keep saying *our?* You are not me! You are nothing but a vacant voice, distracting me from what is really happening. How do I restore my original face?

Turn on the television, Aurora. Maybe then you will see what has become of us.

I hesitate to flick the switch on the television set; I'm entranced by my transparent skin. I can see the pulse of blood, my veins... All the intricacies that make up my material existence.

Turn on the television. Please, Aurora.

I turn it on, not knowing what else to do in the moment, and the warm ambient radiation greets my amber-infused head.

> See, Aurora? That is you. That is me. Observe our bodies, merged as one.

I stare at grainy footage of a man who violates me from behind as I'm pushed over the edge of a sofa. I can almost feel his penis inside of me. My face is how I remember it, but I don't remember him.

> How can you forget me so easily, Aurora? We've been together since the beginning. I used to watch you on a screen very similar to this one.

I press my hands to the smooth, shiny glass of the amber bowl; I yearn to touch my old face.

> We must not dwell on this. Let's keep moving. As I said at the outset, something pursues us.

THE CONCEPT OF OUR GREAT POWER

○ ○

They—The Masses—will find us. Here we become a Goddess.

How do you know? How do you have this knowledge if we've been inseparable?

When they inevitably notice us, the pursuit will begin again.

Again?

We may not remember all the causes, but each successive passage restores the power of the Serpent. Don't you recall our recent mating? **He who will know our Great Power will become Invisible, and the Fire will not be able to consume ~~him~~.** The Serpent, cunning in its ways, knows only three purposes: to corrupt, enslave, and punish those who defy. The secret promises the Serpent made to us are gargantuan, and it is via the gaze of those who have settled here, in the Second Ring, that the Serpent seeks to regain ownership of our soul. Can you feel its presence?

Yes, I definitely feel something. I feel like it's right behind us, and it gets closer as we move to the Centre. But how did we assume this form upon our arrival here?

Our form is insignificant; we've assumed many forms through the course of time and in the breadth of space. **Next: the psychic aeon. It is a small one, and it is mixed with bodies by lodging in the souls and defiling them...**

We can't stay here much longer, Aurora. We're going to have to show ourselves.

Then let's move quickly, even if we have to go further down this spiral. The air is different here, and the buildings—the lights—are all-encompassing and radiate an intense energy I have not felt before.

You must forget about the *I* and say *we*, Aurora. It has always only been *we*. There is no singular. Multiplicities have brought us to this point.

Yet you are sleeping, dreaming dreams. Wake up and return, taste and eat the true food!

They—The Masses—await us, Aurora, just as the Serpent does. We must prepare for broad assaults as we descend further into the core of the Second Ring.

Keep speaking, so I know that you're here.

Sun Drugs

○   ○

"There she is! Look at her!"

We descend the final step of a long stone walkway spiralling down a steep embankment. A throng of ghostly people, their eyes deeply set, look at us with surprise.

Can you see them?
Of course. Your eyes are my eyes. It's just like I told you: they await our arrival.
What should we do? They look at us with unsettling fascination!

"She has finally found us! Gather 'round and bring the Powder!"

A woman steps toward us. The large Sun tattooed on her throat is reflective of the intense heat and power she radiates. Golden hair cascades to Her shoulders; Her fingers run softly over our transparent skin. She smiles widely.

She knows us from a time and place beyond our memory, but her touch is familiar. Let her caress us so we can regain our deepest memories.
Her touch is electrifying... It heals. Our hand feels different now.
Yes, the growth of new nerve endings can be seen in our fingertips: new blood vessels have begun to form.

"The Goddess has answered our prayers and returned! Let us take Her to Her rightful throne!"

We're being lifted onto their shoulders. Where are they taking us?

Let's stay silent for the moment and see where this leads. If nothing else, in the light of the Sun, we can avoid the Serpent's essence.

Is it day? It's hard to tell from this depth, but the vast luminescence of the neon glow manages to find its way down to here, wherever we may be.

"Give Her the Formula; it's her godly right to know!"

They're going to give us the combination of items that go into the dream powder as a gift of gratitude for our return to their space. Once they set us down, we will consume their offering.

They have plans for us beyond the Soma that they've prepared for our return. Our arm regains some level of substance as the skin regrows over the transparent barrier that holds our body together. We will drink when the Formula has been committed to memory.

You forget that this formula was committed to our memory long ago; this is a reenactment, a test of us as a valid Goddess-Form.

They will place us at the foot of a massive tower. Here we will search our mind palace for the sacred pledge they seek.

"Bring Her the Formula, and let Her taste!"

We raise our hand to silence them and finally speak.

"The Formula is as follows: Ten parts hibiscus is the Sun itself at the Centre. Ten parts chamomile is the Moon in the sky. Five parts jasmine is Venus, love exalted. Two parts mint is the massive Jupiter, while two parts cannabis is the dense Saturn. One part ginger is the warlike Mars, and five parts cassia is equal to the messenger Mercury."

They bow with their heads to the ground.

We drink as they carry us away.

THE DAUGHTERS OF QUIET MINDS

o o

I still persist, but *We* spin. The gracious, celebratory crowd sets us down outside a tower that leads to the surface of the Ring. A divine magnificence pulses within, sending bliss from head to loin.

> Look ahead! A group exits the tower to greet us; they carry razor garlands and fresh fruit and lay them in our path.
> Two females come through the crowd... *We* know them—or *I* knew them.

One in orange, one in purple—they carry mother-of-pearl staves. They say nothing. Motioning, they request that we place our head into their waiting hands. We are detained by our new followers as the female clad in purple unsheathes a small saw, previously hidden inside her staff.

> What are they going to do to us?
> I don't know, but we must be still.

The crowd holding us vibrates subtly as the women approach.

> "Our Mother has finally returned. Let the Cosmic Saw slowly crack the mind open."

The Divine Formula rises. We feel it. We watch the saw blade pierce the edge of the amber shell in which our head is encased; the fluid drains, and the crowd falls to their knees, lapping the liquid with their waiting tongues.

These women have our Eye, dilated to bring in the Light.

Their hands are warm as they each grab half of the amber; it is slowly pulled apart. Our Head is finally free, and our damp hair hangs limply; the crowd milks it with their mouths as we're carried away.

"Take our mother to the Temple of the Serpent where she shall, once again, ascend in splendour!"

SERPENT PARASOL

o   o

The two halves of the amber shell are carried on a small pedestal. Within the temple walls, the neon light becomes passive—it is sufficient to create perfect shadows, but not bright enough to fully illuminate the Chambers through which we proceed. The journey has ended; the place of worship awaits us.

I am of perfect mind, and rest... I am honoured and praised and scornfully despised.

I—Eye—Left Path—There is no difference now.

"Aurora," one says from behind a black veil. "This is the realm of the dead; here the serpent *truly* lives."

Illumined by our mental solar barque, we see.

I have forgotten where I am and who I am. I am hanging in nothing.

The Daughters guide us down a long hallway to an open area with a high vaulted ceiling and a black and white checkered floor bordered with gold.

We can feel the vibration of the serpent as we move deeper into these Chambers.
You will surely not die.

The Daughters smile timidly as we are directed to an opening at the Chamber's end.

We should ask what lies beyond.

Yes, but would they even tell us?

Let's look ahead as they open the final door. In the distance, there is someone—a creature?—high atop a stone platform; they are illuminated by a neon green light.

The Daughters and the entourage stop, split apart, and motion at us to move forward.

"Aurora, take this amber shell that we have removed from your Head. Present it to the Serpent. He will know you, for as you vibrate in his presence, he vibrates in yours."

The Formula has truly taken hold now due to its pureness of form, and we cannot resist this encounter.

Aurora, I've waited patiently for you. I am the Monad, the Aion Teleos. Come to me with that withered shell, and kiss my lips once more.

Paranoia Inlay

o   o

He (It?) wears a blood cravat around his reptile neck. We are naked; the entirety of our transparent flesh, given life by the Daughters, grows thick and dense in his (Its?) grip.

Look down: the throng of followers watches this quiet regeneration/assault.

"Do you remember when I was nothing more than a creature crawling on my belly, Aurora? Do you remember me?"

His (Its) smooth, spiked hemi-penis grows larger inside us—inhuman hands grip our arms tightly behind us as he savours the amniotic fluid still sticking throughout our stringy hair. The scent emanating from his (Its) skin adds a degree of delirium to the Formula surging through our veins.

Om namo narayanaya, Om namo narayanaya…

"My mate, Aurora. What lives within you, that voice you always hear, is now also mine. We will grow together indefinitely: powerful, proud… Resonant in every movement of our limbs and our collective voice."

He (It) moves deeper and faster. Lights change colour, flash, burn out retinas. The crowd below us cheers. They fall to their knees: wailing, praying, embracing, kissing. He (It) is in full rhythm now. The fullness of his serpent member releases his seed deep into us. Warm limbs quiver, and our muscles tense around the foreign reptilian cock. Serpent hands encircle our throat; pleasure splits the space between our eyebrows.

Obelisk

○   ○

"Lie there, Aurora, and let us teach you. Don't turn your head. Keep your eyes closed. The Godhead has been fused to your being, but your body must finish reanimating."

"??"

"You have entered the space of the Obelisk, built by the Orphic Doctors—master herbalists who developed the True Formula for what the profane call 'dream powder.' You, Aurora—the messenger and communicator—are the bridge among all the Rings; we've been patiently awaiting your return, your coronation, your Saturnalia, and your feast."

"My Sisters? What happened to them when I arrived here?"

"They were the first to follow you, and we are their Daughters—the offspring of generations of ascetic women who nurtured their daughters and murdered their sons. The Obelisk is the only remnant of a time before we were separated from the Centre by borders."

"The Centre is where I should go."

"No one goes there. It is forbidden, even for you. That is the Godhead's original nest."

"For me, everything is permitted."

"Listen carefully, Aurora. Your Ascension is complete. You have returned *here,* where you rightfully belong. There is no need to go any further; there is only uncertainty beyond this Ring. This Obelisk, like many others beyond this plane, is a marker for the dead. We stand above them, ready to be received into the blinding light that you are sure to bring."

What she is saying is a concern to us, isn't it? We do not know the dimensions of the time and space we are in, so how can they expect us to be calm to their warning?

Nothing is forbidden to us. They only say these things to protect us, but did we ask for this? No. We're confused as to where our body is...

In their imperishable unity, the pyramids—endlessly— continue to crystallize the mobile succession of the Ages. Do you hear me clearly now, Aurora?

"What you need now is to rest here, in the Chamber, without distraction. The Formula will run its course, and your flesh will fully regenerate to the golden sheen we aspire to see. This space is all things, Aurora: Temple, Obelisk, Chamber—a sacred Triad that will be revealed to you through the journey you're about to take with us."

They're turning off all the lights, and here we all lay together as one, with and against the other. Is this who we really are? This combination of disparate voices alone in one body?

This feels familiar... It is here where we used to kiss and caress, forget madness and decay as the day receded into night; it was here that the winds gently swept down to the river and gave us pause as we looked up at the rising lunar disk. Now we've returned?

Neon Palms in Milky Moonlight
(Preamble)

o   o

"The Procession, which begins at the entrance to the Chamber where the Blessed One sleeps, will ascend through the seven levels and conclude on the street where the multitudes await Her revival. First, She will be awakened after her regenerative sleep and cleansed in the Hall of the Root, where the faithful go to scatter their anxieties and fears. The Daughters will then sacrifice a virgin boy from the Ring and anoint her legs in his blood.

The ascent will continue to the Sacral Interior Gate. Here the Blessed One will be clothed in an orange robe embroidered in gold to match the sheen of Her newly glowing skin. A small group of the chosen will adhere to the rule of law and let the Blessed One pleasure them with her tongue before she departs upward.

The Room of Yellow, just above the sacral gate, is an important one; it is the midway point. It is here where kisses are placed on Her heart by Her followers. She will then choose one to accompany her through the levels that lead back to the living world.

The Blessed One alone will enter the Great Hall of Vibration. She will pause at its centre; a series of dungchen will wail, stimulating her vocal cords atrophied after years of neglect. The arousal of these cords will imbue her with incredible power.

As the brightness begins to creep in through the tempered purple glass of the Eye Chamber—the true home of the Blessed one and her original place of rest—it is said our future Queen will be privy to visions when entering and settling in this space, and it is here where She will truly see again, throngs of people cheering above her. The Blessed One will give a sign as to when she will move upward to finish Her ascent.

By the time the veil separating the lower realm from the highest is finally lifted, Her followers will have surely flogged themselves, sacrificed their first-born sons, and prepared wreaths in Her honour. She will exit onto a balcony overlooking the streets of bright neon gloss and artificial waterfalls, don her crown of obsidian, and watch the Ritual of the Swallowing... For now, we will wake Her from her regenerative sleep so the formalities can begin.

Do you hear us, Blessed Aurora? Awaken from your healing slumber! Cast off the shell of the subconscious! Meet your followers; they have waited all these years for your return. We chant in unison to wake you beneath the full moon that serves as the alternate shadow that brought you to us. The glowing palms above you shine brightly with light. Can you hear the distant voices of the many Daughters wailing and crying in your name?"

"Wake, Aurora! Wake!"

QUARTZ SAFARI
(HALL OF THE ROOT)

∘　∘

S iO$_2$—the walls of amethyst shine like lavender; it's almost blinding, and it's certainly beautiful...

Bits of citrine seem to make up the spaces in between. Hands lift our naked body. Every touch feels like velvet across our new skin.

"Is there a mirror to see what we have become after this heavy narcotic sleep?"

Someone assures us that we will be able to see the results after the sacrifice—an animal?

They are bringing in a blindfolded boy. He shakes with fear. He pisses all over himself. What is the purpose of all this? Can we intervene?

They will allow no interference on our part; this is their Way, their tradition to mark our return. The Daughters surround him.

The followers are let into the Hall and are told to stand aside as the death instrument is brought forward.

Let's plug our ears and close our eyes, for this is certain to be awful, bloody, and tragic.

Where has our collective spirit toward sacrificial violence gone? They are doing this for *US*, to forge a new covenant with *THEM*.

Let us watch with rapt attention as they sharpen the quartz knife before his eyes—the fear that runs through his body has slowed, perhaps because he has accepted his fate.

The Daughters tightly grip his hair and limbs while a cantor chants loudly.

A clean cut across the throat—the tiny body spasms, and the blood is carefully collected in a small chalice. The death rattle follows quickly, and a group of onlookers are poised to mutilate the corpse.

The chalice, held by a steady hand, approaches...

"Aurora, please accept this sacrificial blood and cover your legs and loins in his essence!"

In an attempt to Purge
(The Sacral Interior Gate)
○ ○

"Lead the Blessed one in. Clothe Her golden skin."

Our eyes no longer deceive us. Look at all the monuments, statues, and fountains adorned with naked forms: beautiful bronze-skinned females recline on these objects—their legs are spread wide, as if to receive us.

The Daughters outfit us with a robe of orange and gold, **and do not fear those who kill the body but not the soul. Rather, fear Him who can destroy both body and soul.**

"Spread your lips and let your Queen feast on your flesh."

The inner ghost wants to die within us. Aurora of three voices enmeshed in one golden body: We shall put our tongue onto the pleasure point and rid ourself of depraved dreams and sickly thoughts.

Never before have we been drawn to female flesh in this manner. Look at them, so quiet and still, their flowers in bloom... It draws the nectar of desire into our mouth.

Run our hands over their buttocks and the sides of their torso. Spread our fingers across their warm breasts; our tongue, newly moist, rests itself on the pearl.

Each one tastes different, swells between our teeth; their eyes look into ours like the communion between sets of stars. Our lips are frosted with the love fluid of the yoni, rejecting the lingam—at least for the time being. **There are then nine kinds of union according to dimensions; the horse and deer form the highest union...**

"Send our Queen upwards! She has slaked her thirst between the thighs of the sacred."

THE BRIDE STRIPPED BARE
(THE ROOM OF YELLOW)
o o

Majestic yellow, almost gold—like us—so bright that even the most devoted followers shield their eyes as they enter.

The taste of a dozen dampened flowers clings to our lips as our skin melds with the exuberant colour.

We will sink into the background as the Daughters prepare what they refer to as "the Kissing of the Heart." **There are no eyes, ears, nose, tongue, body, or thoughts. There are no forms, sounds, scents, tastes, sensations; no field of vision, and no realm of thought.** Let them tear the clothes from our newly minted golden skin and lay us gently on that giant slab of granite before they kiss between our breasts like the Daughters direct them to do. They bite and lick! Their warm breath dampens our flesh.

We see an obsessive obedience pulse in their eyes as they place their moistened lips on ours without permission; enraptured, drugged on pure Formula, they kiss all parts of us now, inserting fingers into ass and vagina alike. **Because in emptiness there is no form, sensation, conception, synthesis, or discrimination.**

The Daughters order the followers to cease their actions and kneel around the granite slab: *We* must be clothed in regalia for the continuing ascent. They direct us to choose someone—*the one*—from this lusty throng. The chosen one will follow us upward, toward the holographic light and false sky.

There is definitely one that is above all the rest: it is the first. She pushed her way to the front, defying the throng to kiss our face and warm our beating heart. The woman with the emerald-coloured hair and slender fingers... *She* is the one. **Since there are no obstructions, they have no fears. Because they are unattached to backward dream thinking, their final result is Nirvana.**

HOLOGRAPHIC SNOWFALL
(THE GREAT HALL OF VIBRATION)
o   o

"Our Queen must pass through a vibration of 2.5Hz as she enters the hall through the channel of the winter hologram. The vibrations will relax her prior to reaching the rotunda, where she will hear the sacred dungchens being blown by males in the sacred place. She will then kneel and open her mouth, thus liberating her vocal cords for the waves that will shake her deeply. Bring in our Queen!"

The hall is built with acoustic perfection; it amplifies and funnels the sound waves. Even our thoughts vibrate to the distant sound of the dungchens.

We must brace ourselves as we travel deeper: we don't know the effect the waves will have on our newly trans-formed body, regardless of what *they* say.

Look at how the light changes as we approach! Shifting white shades turn into snowflakes that are not really there but fall on us just the same.

"The Queen arrives! Begin the ceremony; we will depart, and she will have run of this sacred space, built for her while we awaited her return."

The dungchens sound as Aurora enters the rotunda.

A great shimmer runs over our golden skin. A pulse widens and deepens within us; it centers in our throat and gently shakes the vocal cords with each step we take to the center of the rotunda. Let us get on our knees, awash in the bath of sound.

We must now open our mouth wide and release the words hidden inside us to the masses who await our proclamation.

"~~He~~ masters all states and arrives at the opposite shore as an equal of all past, present, and future. ~~He~~ displays his wondrous appearance in a sublime body. ~~He~~ emits a thousand beams of untainted light. Worlds in the ten directions are shaken without exception, but not one sentient being is terrified. Although sentient beings are innumerable, ~~he~~ enables them all to end their evils and afflictions..."

The sound of the voice is so deep and tremendous that instantly the bones of the dungchen players shatter and the skin is flayed from their faces by the reverberations in the Great Hall; they scream in agony before falling dead from the intense blast.

Look at what we have unleashed with the inner voice that attached itself to us! Its power is amplified, and our collective throat is clear and strong! Bloody essence clings to our golden skin from the explosion of flesh and bone, but the Daughters arrive to cleanse our skin once more before adorning us with our sacred garments.

"Admit the deeply faithful into this Chamber so they can see the aftermath of their Queen's wrath. Inhabitants of the Second Ring will hear these words as their sovereign inches closer. The woman with the emerald hair shall lead her Queen through the final rooms, into the blazing bright streets!"

DEAD ZONE
(THE EYE CHAMBER)
o   o

S he is truly beautiful.

The air is silent as we are escorted into the Chamber; our heart beats wildly as she clasps her ivory hand around ours, surrounded by the stillness of a thousand graves.

> What is this place we have stepped into with no preparation?
>
> But we *are* prepared!

If our golden skin had hair, it would prickle with goose flesh from her soft touch and the thought that we are now walking over the dead.

> The only light seems to come from a small section in the vaulted stone ceiling.
>
> She inches closer; her breath is warm as she whispers into our ear.

> ### "Look up into the purple light as I place this Formula tablet on your tongue, my Queen."

The taste is familiar, sweet like honey. The swirling purple light pulses with increasing intensity as we stare deeper into its depths; a transparent lotus appears at its core.

> She is on her knees now. She caresses our thighs, opens our robe, and lightly kisses our skin. She inches up slowly...
>
> Her tongue is soft and moist; it finds its way into our

depths—ass and birth canal; it laps at the swollen seed growing beneath her ministrations.

Grab her emerald hair and press her harder into us—quickly! The purple light grows more dense and bright.

Images form and fade.

Her tongue moves faster!

Our grip tightens around her head to the distant chants of the crowd.

Distorted faces of the dead mutate as the pleasurable tremors blaze hotly through our newly grown nerves. Our strength rises. We squeeze her skull, overcome, but she refuses to stop, deeply in trance.

Our eyes, once so dull, now see past, present, and future. Let us apply pressure to her temples until blood runs from her ears!

She gives us a final smile as her body goes limp. Our fingers drip with her blood, and we watch it mix with her green trellises.

New Dawn

(Coronation)

○ ○

"**P**repare the balcony suite! Our Queen will soon ascend the staircase. Her footsteps approach. Ready the virgin boys on the street below for sacrifice. She will have a clear view of her subjects!"

From toes to crown, our body vibrates with pleasure—it tingles and pulses with a newly awakened energy.

The Daughters impatiently watch us enter the blinding light. They offer us their hands; two others stand by the edge of the balcony, holding an obsidian crown.

Our hands are slick with the blood of the emerald woman; let us anoint their faces.

"Our Queen! You honour us all with this blood. Gaze upon the faithful, and see what they have done for you on this, the most glorious of days!"

Thousands of lotus petals have been strewn through the streets amidst the blinding holographic lights of the Ring. Interspersed among the petals are a hundred bloody heads of young boys. Their eyes are closed, and their heads sit atop wooden stakes, veins and arteries dangling like ribbons. In the distance, a huge bonfire has been lit; the corpses have been thrown in piles, driving the stench of death through the open air.

Shall we address them?

The Daughters want to clothe us with a fresh train of sensuous, deep purple satin. Our skin gleams and reflects the photon overload below us. The Sun feels so very near that we could kiss it with our new, well-formed lips...

> Let us speak from the depths like we did in the Great Hall of Vibration; we shall see how wide and powerful our voice has become with the essence of the serpent in our belly.

The Daughters shout to the clamouring crowds below: "Your Queen!"

The shouting and violence are incessant as we approach the parapet in our regal attire.

"Let silence be the first documented act of our reign. **Vayu, let fleet-footed coursers bring thee speedily to our feast, to drink first of the juice we pour, to the first draught of Soma! May our glad hymn, discerning well, uplifted, gratify thy mind. Come with thy team-drawn car, O Vayu, to the gift, the sacrificer's gift!"**

The shockwave from Aurora's throat fans the flames of the fires below; citizens are set ablaze, and those closest to the blast of words are maimed or disintegrate instantly. Below the Queen: panic, disorder, and chaos. People run in all directions. Blood and bits of flesh cling to their skulls. They scream in pain and anguish and wonder what they did to anger their newly-crowned Queen. Aurora observes the scene with indifference, then returns to the corridors of the Obelisk with the Daughters.

Kozyrev Mirrors

o   o

After a period of three days—dubbed "the Incubation" by the Daughters—we are set to enter the long-sealed Hypomagnetic Chamber beneath the Hall of the Root, a sacred place to ward off the effects of the subtle waves of the Sun.

The Daughters speak to us in hushed tones.

"This space beneath the Obelisk—a primal antithesis to the Ascendant Staircase—was built by the Ophic Doctors* to house our Queen upon her return. This will be your permanent residence, and we will attend to you here."

The Daughters are attempting to hold us here, in another formative Chamber. Have we not had enough of these places of concealment? Our true birthright lies beyond this Ring—in the First—where we have been forbidden to tread. Maybe we should rouse them to the idea, now that we are fully in control of the situation here. Though, how can we be fully in control? They expect us to remain in this Chamber forever.

"Daughters! Come stand before us. We must speak with you!"

"Yes, what is it, our Queen? Are you dissatisfied with something in this Chamber?"

"The problem is your expectation that we will remain here indefinitely. We must go to the First Ring. When all the affairs are complete here, we will finish what we set out to do."

"With all due respect, our Queen, we cannot allow that to happen. Your presence here is all too important. When the Orphic Doctors built this Obelisk, it was expected that our Queen would assume the throne upon her return, and her prescience would guide us into the future. At the rear of this Chamber is a group of Kozyrev Mirrors; they will allow you to amplify your foretold latent psychic abilities."

Somewhere in the wild swirl of memory, where the fragments of a former life reside, we find truth in their words. If our body is no longer the same, how can the mind be in the same state? Do we know what hides beneath the surface of our thoughts?
Let us enter this collection of mirrors; we will test the accuracy of their prediction. Perhaps we can see the end of our stay here.

"Follow us now, our Queen, to the centre of the mirror cluster. Here you will find a space for your comfortable repose. We will initiate a vibrational sequence; once we are assured you are in the proper elevated state, it will amplify over the course of a few hours. Enter at your leisure."

Aurora enters and disrobes, her golden skin reflecting back at her from the large, strategically angled aluminium cylinders. She closes her eyes, and almost immediately the corners of the Chamber begin to emit a deep hum. Within minutes, she is submerged in a growing field of sound. She abandons her senses and cracks the barrier between her mind and the veil that shields a thousand secret pathways.

DEATH OF ORION

o o

Mind propulsion/dissolution.

Can you feel it consume us? Have we dissolved?

Animals and noisy flowers in the distance, like static—their forms are not real, but they beg us to touch them.

They are trying to speak to us—the plants too. It is as though a flow of invisible words attempts to reach us through this barrier, whatever it is.

It is the barrier of the Second Ring which blocks us from the healing energy of the Sun. **The purpose of all this is neither to bury Orion nor to praise it—it is to tell the story for the first time and the facts surrounding its life and death, and to explain as fairly as possible the philosophical issues which are involved with its Fate...**

How have we gained this knowledge?

We gleaned this knowledge through events in the past. We can watch them unfold in the hollow of space afforded by the mirrors. Let's look at what we have gained from this propulsion and dissolution.

Look there! Who are those faceless beings? They form a circle and turn their faceless heads to the sky. There is one among them who appears different from the rest. **We, as singular entities, know this person; we were all this person, or so we would like to believe. At the end of a cycle, you return—if not to the starting point, then at**

**least to something inaugural, which may be something
very intense.**

Can they hear our thoughts across this field of space?

They do not listen. They are more concerned with
elevating their spirits to the radiating globe, which is our
ultimate destination. **We must kill the inner circle of this
deformed, soulless Ring. In doing so, we will reacquire
our birthright.**

We, too, must die by someone's hand. Look carefully at
the scene unfolding! The unique one bears their naked
flesh to a huntress, who pierces their heart and throat
with poisonous arrows from her bow. The faceless beings
bow to her.

This is how it all began, and this is how it Ends. Amor Fati.

TRANQUILITY WAVES

○ ○

"Our Queen, we have reserved our decision about you leaving the Ring until the day after your Feast Night. We hope that is adequate."

Should we let them live until then or disintegrate them now? Either way... However, we are inclined to do it now. The feast is just a distraction before they tell us that we will not be allowed to move forward. **Gather them together, and our voice will be subtle and powerful, like a warm wind that gently shakes the branches before the leaves come tumbling down.**

"Gather in a circle, my Daughters, and listen to your Queen speak. Though you may feel confused by the sound of a foreign tongue, rest assured that her message will be clear."

"If we may? There is a matter that needs attention before we prostrate ourselves before you. Please follow us back to the Eye Chamber; we must bestow an ancient object upon you."

Is this a deception? Why have they waited until exiting the Chamber to tell us about this object?
Our mind has expanded—they sense something, but it's a mere tickle, not even a premonition. It is a single molecule drifting in vast open space. We must keep our thoughts as quiet as possible within the sacred walls... Until the final moment.

A fool, overwhelmed by ignorance, thinks of the body as beautiful. But when it lies dead, swollen and discoloured, cast away in a cemetery, it is disregarded.

Does this feel different? The air has changed since we last exited this Chamber.

The Daughters turn slowly toward us. Their collective lips become terse as a small panel opens on the far wall.

"Behold, our Queen—your true sceptre. It has been awaiting your arrival since the construction of the Obelisk. It is an item of power; the Orphic Doctors believed it would one day be yours."

Encrusted with neither jewels nor gold, the scepter is a jade-handled blade three feet in length, beautiful and elegant.

Look at how it shimmers and vibrates as we approach.
The Daughters surround us: they can feel our thoughts.
Not for much longer! We shall sing them the song of death, then take the weapon.

"We know your plan, our Queen, and we cannot allow you to abandon this Ring. The First Ring is forbidden to *all!*"

"Ooooooooooommmmmm, tryambakam yajamahe sugandim pusti-vardhanam urvarukam iva bandhanam mrtyor muksiya ma mrtat!"

Look at their skin bubble before it sloughs off their muscles!
They are frozen where they stand.
We have shown them gentleness and mercy, despite their disobedience.

"Farewell! Ooooooooommmmmm, tryambakam yajamahe sugandim pusti-vardhanam urvarukam iva bandhanam mrtyor muksiya ma mrtat..."

They are dust.

ALICE IN MY FANTASIES

○　　○

The air is charged with a fierce energy—our energy, free at last! Who remains in opposition?

Let's not forget that we had an intent, nearly forgotten, to seek the precious mystery of the First Ring. Though, as we step through the dust of the Daughters, we feel a longing that has existed since the beginning, whenever that was, and has culminated within this new body. **With no hate in the mind, the journey's end was reached safely. And while in the form of the royal serpent, no hate sprang to mind while being cruelly treated by the snake charmer. Before we move toward the boundaries of this Ring**, we must empty our spirits by revisiting the touch, the feel, **and the pain of others.** We must duplicate the intensity that we found with the emerald-haired woman. May her spirit be restless and sting us with pleasure.

There is rustling outside, and in low whispers, the servants ask where the Daughters are...

"Come forward, you cowards and lowly servants, and prostrate yourself before your Queen."

Look at them shuffle with fear; they tremble and cry for our forgiveness. We must set them the task of preparing for our departure.

"Fetch the body of the Emerald woman! Collect the dust of the

Daughters from the floor of this Chamber and gather all the reserves of the Formula in this Ring! It is time for your Queen to cross a forbidden frontier so she can be free once more. But first, a celebration of the flesh is in order!"

THE NIGHT OF THE FEAST

o   o

The dining hall overlooking the centre of the Ring radiates with row upon row of deep neon fuzz. Our skin reflects the glow back to our newly grown eyes in shimmering shades. A tug on the leash, and the servant licking between our rear cleft brings back those first memories.

> They feel like first memories, but something within us feels older, primal, beyond our scope.
>
> The pleasure is the same without question—the uninhibited lust/love of a time... removed?

Our servants pour large cylinders of Formula collected around the Ring into a large communal bowl; they slake their collective thirst and convulse on the floor in ecstasy.

> **It is time to make our entrance... And our exit.**

"Gather around those of you who have not yet had the opportunity to pleasure your Queen in earnest. Come and suck on our flesh; become holy and blessed!"

> Look at them scramble! See the man and woman whose eyes are tuned to ours? They want to approach us, but their fear is palpable.
>
> They look delectable. They will do nicely to satisfy our desires before the feast begins.

"You two there! Approach us slowly, and strip off your clothes. You will be our concubines on this glorious night as we celebrate

our forthcoming freedom from the oppression of this Ring!"

They waste no time. The woman slips her hands under the thin fabric and kneads our golden breasts. Exquisite feelings are intensified by her cool lips; they pause at our nipples; her tongue takes its time with each one...

> This male is also thorough; he kneels before us and presses his face between our thighs while a dozen servants put the finishing touches on the feast. Our main course will be served soon, and we can finally shed these creatures and this Ring from our consciousness for good.
>
> A group of them are bringing out the main course now. **The body of the emerald woman has been placed in the centre of the banquet table, surrounded by the dust of the Daughters and the massive bowls of Formula.**

"Come, my servants. Let us partake of the flesh and the divine Soma together, if only once!"

The concubines wipe their mouths on the hem of Aurora's gown, then sit on the floor, cross-legged. A servant hands their Queen a narrow wooden pipe; she uses it to snort the ashes of the Daughters before she sits gracefully, all eyes on her movements. She lifts the jade-handled sword as it's presented to her and proceeds to chop at the remains of the emerald woman with quick, careful blows. She motions to her subjects, indicating they are to eat from the corpse and drink. They tear at the flesh with relish, the Formula dripping from their chins. Aurora smiles, then quickly swallows a large chalice of Formula. She kisses her concubines on the lips, then departs, sword in hand. She makes her way out of the dining hall and down the stairwell, into the neon clusters of the streets. No one notices. By the time anyone is aware of her absence, Aurora has already crossed over the boundary of the Ring.

PART FIVE
THE BOOK OF SOYGA

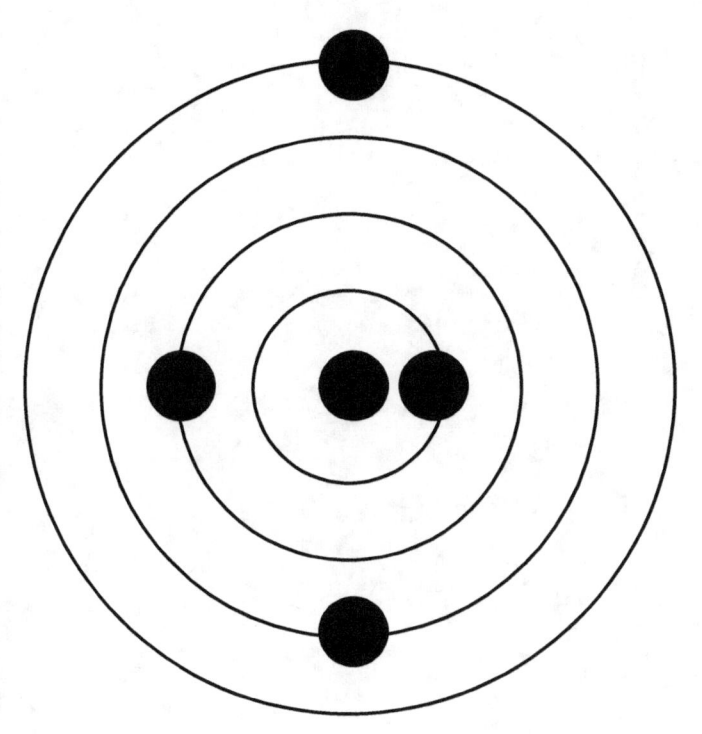

THE VENT

○

Abundance of shadows—*I* is never a sufficient pronoun when used to describe my malady, but *I* have been down here for some time, though my sense of time's movement has been washed away by my isolation in this stone Chamber. The Tribe, clothed in dark-coloured emblems, settled in the curved stadiums and connecting passageways of the obsidian prison. *They* call it "the Vent," an extinct geyser where they make small fires for warmth; a wealth of lunar mansions and stars on the ruby plateau glitter above me. The Tribe lives a kilometre away, and they await my return. My inner vision tells me I have returned many times before. Through the hollow of the natural formations, I hear a hiss and the other voice.

Look at the Towering Obelisk, the *blind infernal extravagance of the Sun.* **The Solar Kiss. Burn our lips against her golden flesh; it guides us toward one another. Seek the Solar Kiss. In the Sixteenth episode (in the future, where we will all be conjoined), you can hear a voice ask, as he makes a leap of faith, the eternal question: Why?** *The obscurity of a mystery comes from images that something akin to a lucid dream borrows from the realm of the crowd.* **The trauma of being alive does not equate to the enormous trauma of realizing that you have always been alive, in some form or another.**

Knowledge knows no enemy other than ignorance. What is revealed in deserts and other wide open spaces guides us back to the beginning. Here we were one—before all this, in the great Cosmic echo chamber, where words did not exist. *Deus Primus, Deus Secundus, Deus Tertius—a tripartite Entity, birthed in the Void.* Seek the origin of the substance the old ones call

"Formula" or "the powder of Projection." This substance induces dreams of walking among pine trees, by mountain lakes, and in spaces where vague spiritual remnants float about, terrorizing the living from the vantage point of the fourth dimension. *This section takes up Earth, spread throughout the Universe.*

EYES OF THE SHAMAN

o

The Seer is a conduit across all fields of space and time. Magnetic tape gave birth to an image on 1400 feet of material that played through a box transmitting a grainy signal whose origin dates back to the Beginning... Die Tür ist Offen. A.'s (our) moans are the primordial OM reduced to a slower length and pitch. She speaks to us with a siren song that shatters our material body. Her power extends across all instruments of destruction and all instruments of light; it sears the eyes of those who look upon her. She has many names and identities and lies in hiding, waiting for us to find her again.

I awake from a deep slumber, and beams of light pass through the hollows of the Chambers, signalling that another day has begun. Climbing onto the ruby plateau, I see the Tribe in the distance, preparing for my return. I rub my hands together and place them on my eyes—portals to the deepest, most obscure parts of a person. The Tribe fears me because they know that I can see their pasts and futures. With a piece of smoothed glass, I send a signal of my imminent descent. They signal back. Directing my face to the Sun, the morning begins in silence.

Our body moves, unbidden, to the primordial pulse. We coalesce into the rhythm that courses through nature—the hypnotic trance of the infinite. The fractal box of reality provides no refuge, leaving us with nothing but kinetic energy directed toward the Void. Our words fall like feathers, and we are cocooned together in a verbal caress. *The power, the clear one of clear ones, is a thousand times brighter than the Sun.* Must we always spin in circles, always return to the point of origin? We have grown tired together, but we have been tired since the beginning, which was so long ago. When will we be free of the repetition of the cosmic song?

You Disappear

○

Yes, the *you* will disappear—an inevitable fading out of character, collapsing into the great miasma of pure being. Currently suppressed in your mind are the lustful tremors that draw you closer to the Centre. In a fearful tunnel where spectres and demons reside, someone or something said: *The Allegorist is the opposite of the Collector.* You hear my voice like you can hear the other; it is the deep hiss that

echoes on the opposite side of your brain and speaks these words that nestle deep in your groin: *Lust is the quest of the Flesh for the Unknown.* You feel me there, waiting to burst into the open. Pure potential becomes a loving embrace.

They—The Tribe—worship the Black Cube with its latent energies, its density, its mass. It is the Age of Saturn, the time where I was conceived and born in the House of Aaton. As they bow and pledge allegiance to me, they plan a sacrifice for my reawakening. You can hear me... They worship me, but you can hear my voice hissing in your ear. I am ERM. Lift your head from deep contemplation and focus your energies on me, for only through me will your power come to fruition. Go to those below. Tell them that you have heard my voice from beyond and learned of my presence and all that it will entail.

Locking myself in the underground with the vapours from deep cavernous springs has made my inner vision strong. I feel the serpent's breath; it acts like a psychotropic mist. I can smell its cold blood mix with mine across the divide. To pray to this creature is an act of submission, yet every time I open my eyes and the Sun blinds me with its rays, I also feel the pull of tender vaginal walls, though I made a pledge to never embrace another woman. She follows me, infiltrates my dreams, and contaminates my thoughts with erotic gestures. I shake these visions; I know I may fall prey to her again, she who lives in the shifting colours of the night sky. She hears me now and forever.

THE HACKED AND GNAWED

O

Days and nights run together in a series of repeated images. After the hundredth day has passed, my thoughts begin to sink and settle, but the voices continue to chatter on the fringes. While I sit in the moonlight, eyes closed, a gentle wind passes across my face; I look down into the valley. The Tribe has kindled a large fire, and they are roasting a body over the open flames. The Black Cube throbs with a sonic pulse that I can feel, even at this elevation. It runs through me while the fragrant bloom of early evening hangs over the burning flesh below. Retreating to the cave, the voices return and my body trembles.

You see me clearly now, inside and to the left, growing, morphing and changing colour, staining you with my presence and coaxing you with my tongue. Like a chameleon, I will remain hidden from you until I make my presence felt. You attempt to hide, but you are not swift or smart enough to avoid my touch. You resist, but something deep within you yearns to touch me, even though I'm physically absent. We must be one with the

Other that also speaks to you in a bold voice: a trinity of force, crossing and dissecting time and space at will. Kiss me in your fevered dreams, and bring me into the land of the living. We have much to give each other.

Below, you see the destruction of the body; the sacrifice in my name disintegrates before your eyes. Before this rapid descent, you witnessed the *gradual dilation and swelling, the close of life as a bellows is with the wind.* You attempt to choose the righteous path; you perceive the body as a simple vessel worth discarding *by its joints, by its openings, by its concavities, and by its gross convexities.* Leave all this contemplation and strangeness behind, and join your brethren who await you below; they yearn for your acknowledgement of my form within the dark Cube. Go to them.

KNOWLEDGE OF DANGER

○

Holy is he who castrates his seed, casting it to the wind or to the ground or upon the flesh it desires. In a time far from now—because I can see all—*a bride brought forth to be married is gloriously adorned in a great variety of precious garments, which by enhancing her beauty render her pleasant in the eyes of the groom...* But the rites of the bridal night she performs unclothed are what she was tasked with at the moment of her birth. I hear her call within you; she also begs to be actualized. Your brethren know the secret, and they wait for you with bated breath, their gazes locked to the sky, awaiting a signal from your den.

The Tribe eat from the charred corpse across many evenings, but now they also consume the sacred fish that swims in the nearby waters. This golden-striped fish has a deep power to affect the mind... I wonder if they have ingested too much of its oils, resulting in the cannibalism that I see. The oil has long served as a means to open the inner eye, but prolonged use leads to intoxication that is often deadly. They are slowly going insane as they revert to a primitive stage. They howl at the rising moon and curse at the stars while dancing around the remnants of the fire. It is unlikely that their howls will die out by dawn. I can feel the other voice rising in me as their devilish laughter begins to infect me too.

You who deny me know the words of an even more ancient entity, one that existed long before this desolation of land and spirit; it resides in text used by its owners for liberation. *In all kinds of becoming, generation, destiny, station, and abode there is not a single formation that he can place his hopes in or hold on to. The three kinds of becoming appear like charcoal pits of* glowing coals, the four primary elements like hideous venomous **snakes**. Saturated with vice, I peer through the haze inside your mind. You secretly crave my disjointed limbs, even as your thoughts dwell in bliss. Isolated and adrift, you rot from within. Do not grapple with me, for you will never win this battle. Not now, not ever.

ACROSS THE DESERTS OF ASH

o

Sitting on the ruby plateau with my (our?) eyes cast downward into the space where the Cube vibrates—the Tribe hums even harder from the ingestion of flesh and sacred fish—my body is overcome by a wave of nausea. My time in the obsidian cave protects me from the evil waves that float across the deserts of ash created by the innumerable sacrifices made by the Tribe as they followed the herds. Only... Since the Cube appeared and the stars aligned, the taste for human flesh has grown stronger within the Tribe. Soon, a time will come when I can no longer shield myself from the power of that object: a mysterious chiselled rock summons me. The intensity of their voices drives me inside the cave to rest.

To deny the power of ERM is to deny a great path forward. In the future, a man will stare into the pink light and be transformed. Buried with his twin sister in the black room of death, he will have gone to rest with secrets known only to the Primordial Ones coiled in the fabric of space. We have witnessed the rise and fall of galaxies and civilizations. Your eyes are my eyes. Your breath is my breath; you feel it across the back of your neck while in deep repose. Succumb. Submit to what wraps around your heart. Shed your skin like I have shed mine so many times before.

You have delighted in solitude and the inner splendour that has been given to you, but you have forsaken the desires of the flesh to see a little further within. The only thing that awakens is the demon dwelling inside; the screams of the damned in the void welcome you home. With my legs splayed across a dozen dimensions, I whisper to you and wonder if you hear my cries. I am the shape, a priestess in the shade. If you follow my voice like a madman chasing a plethora of golden butterflies, you will find my body waiting. At the end of the path, in the perfect altered state, your mind will swim with blue in delirious vertigo as you awaken me once more.

ASTRAL WINDS

○

You seek the function of the Aeon—the root of your journey that has been entirely inward—though through me you have felt the vibrations of another, singing in the back of your skull. *And thereafter madness, all in vain. Thus it has been multiform. How thou hast burned beyond.* You are aware of the Basilisk within the Cube who can only die by seeing its reflection. It seeks to outlive time itself while being bound by its terrible grip, linking beings and non-beings alike. Its veil, thin and tattered, hangs over the many rings that divide up this world and others. *Let him be dedicated, consecrated, blood to blood, heart to heart, mind to mind, none without the circle.*

The blissful, unsettling silence of the morning is a welcome change from the incantations and revelry that accompanied the consumption of human flesh. The Tribe lies on the ground, frothing at the mouth and sitting naked in the trees. I prepare to rejoin them and recall a vision of deep colour and shade where I was instructed to create a divine elixir, drunk by those below in an impure form. The Black Cube hums at a lower vibration. **You hear me now. Step closer. Place your hand upon my surface and listen carefully; I will impart to you the true Formula; the alignment of the stars and planets has manifested me to this time and place. Release all fear and prejudice, and heed my words.**

I am listening without my ears; you exist in the centre of my head, and your voice disperses in rings of vibration. **First, you must be conscious of the times of the year when you collect the ingredients needed for this concoction, spawned from gold and silver by Aforgomon and Azareyhk—cohorts of mine from the veiled realms of Universe B.** Can I trust you to give me the essence that will give me and others the clearest visions of truth? **Before a being such as myself, truth is but a test of one's faith. Lay yourself down, away from the charred flesh and delirium of these Tribesmen, and I will teach you the ways of astral influences so you may teach them.**

Beyond the Plateau

○

There is a saying from a time far removed: *In the sweetest and most gladdening stream flow pure, O Soma, on thy way, pressed out for Indra, for his drink...* Flow onward with thy juice unto the banquet of the Mighty Gods. What this tells you is that the power of the Formula will grant the consumer much in the way of power and insight. As the days become short and the season of Saturn rises, kindle a fire and point to the heavens with your right finger. Softly speak the secret words of this rite: silence and truth. With your hands in the cool earth, make the following design with your fingers: a crescent moon within a square.

Ah, so you have finally fallen prey to the voice of the Basilisk. Do not forget me, my love, for it is you that I seek in the madness of the ethereal space while you seek me in the chamber of your heart, whether you acknowledge it yet or not. It is said that the Bull and Scales yield to the goddess of love, and it is during these times of strangeness, set in the picture of the heavens, that we will come together as one. It is also said that *your words are not supported by the truth, and you travel on crooked ways and desire the wives of others, and in one of them you were given up to death.* I know your thoughts and transgressions, just like the Basilisk that resides in the depths of the Black Cube. Surrender.

For three days, I have stopped trying to silence the voices and instead have grown drunk on their incessant ramblings. I have been chosen to memorize the Formula, imparted to me by the all-powerful ERM, who has made the Tribesmen mad with piercing vibrations. The time has come to leave these empty husks and seek new shelter in the desolate plains where rumours circulate about a hanging garden, the Fava-Rufaida; few have laid eyes on its grotesque features. The Tribesmen, ever severed from reality, do not notice my return or sudden departure from their space; they will surely consume one another, or at the very least, without being aware, murder their brother. Such is the serpent's influence.

DREAM HOUSE

○

The Serpent is not the only being with foresight and hindsight; I have also heard phrases from different epochs, my love. Seek the structure that will combine our forces together in such a way as to transcend any normal conception of time and space. In a distant future, it will be said that *a salient architecture requires, first, the consideration of effects over history and narrative.* The most basic of structures precedes narrative itself and lies somewhere between the Centre and an ever deeper core where walls and columns are be-jewelled with emeralds and diamonds, crafted by an unknown hand in this transparent, distant form. Follow me as you have followed the other.

Aurora, astral partner and rogue lover, speaks a mighty truth despite her physical absence in this field of space. Her message is as clear as mine, as you acknowledge our binding to you. *And into the nothingness came a thought, purposeful and all-pervading, and it filled the Void.* There existed no matter, only force, a movement, a vortex, a vibration of a purposeful thought that filled the Void. Remember this as you pass through the arid lands surrounding the hidden chambers, for only with this in mind will you not perish.

...Countless days have passed since I left the Tribe and the Cube behind, but the voices do not cease. Fatigue is a constant, and I have had very little to eat or drink. I'm hopeful that what little energy I still possess will lead me toward the Hanging Gardens, where my body will finally be shed among the ghosts and desiccated flesh of the past. The air becomes more fragrant and warm the further I go; it warms my bones after many cold nights spent in the obsidian caves of the mountains. My feet guide me far beyond the heavy mist, if death doesn't find me first.

ENTERING THE HALL OF VAPOUR AND LIGHT

○

On the last day, as the final vestiges of energy drained from my exhausted limbs, I felt my eyes were deceiving me. A vast stone structure spread out beneath a canopy of gnarled, overgrown trees and assaulted me with a profound hallucination of vivid colour. It was eerily silent: no animals, no birds, no incessant insects—

only a barely audible hum that seemed to come from underground. The frequency felt similar to the one that emanated from the Black Cube and caused the Tribesmen to break from reality. Questioning why I was exempt from their collective madness, I realized that the seeker gives themselves over to the lightness (or darkness) willingly.

You, my love, will face the shadows of the lower Chambers. Follow my voice, and with each step, I will bring you closer. These words from a future time will speak to your mind: *In the following descent, the Father will appear, and so does the Creator, and then the Creator of all things will come forth.* Here you will find me asleep in my quiet tomb among my protectors, who have called to you in the wilds. The obsidian shielded you from our words until it was time for you to hear us, and the deep green hues of the emerald caves will serve to emancipate you and facilitate our union, as is the natural order of the world we inhabit.

My voice emanates from the Centre; it is here where you will find the solution to your inquiries. You have already taken the first steps beyond this Chamber to complete the process of the true Formula. You will be the first person I impart with this knowledge— use focus to hear my words. Many from the past have ignored these instructions and failed, for the accomplishment of this task requires more than an eagerness; it also requires a lack of ego and submission to my whims. All things consist of three essences, and it is through their painful (but glorious) union that we continue to thrive beyond this time and the next, until we meet each other once more.

WAITING ROOM FOR DEATH

o

Make a small fire in this room. This will be your refuge until you hear me again, demanding you move into the deeper recesses. Prepare the following in a small cauldron, steeped in water, and boiled over the length of the next solar cycle: ten parts of the hibiscus, ten parts chamomile, five parts jasmine, two parts mint, two parts from the sativa plant, one part ginger, and five parts cassia. While the ingredients boil, create a large circle around yourself and remain centred inside it until the Solar Cycle is complete. The Formula will have completed its initial stage, and more time will be needed for it to cool. This is the beginning of the Prothesis that you are to follow.

Every descent, no matter how smooth or uneventful, is full of trepidation and an expectation of death from an unknown factor of nature. I disperse my fear through the fire like the spirit guide suggested; illuminating the darkness calms me as I prepare the concoction, then stretch out my body, my tired bones sinking into the stone. Ever so naturally, I drift...

Close your eyes, my love, and allow my voice to permeate the centre of your thoughts. Recite the following, and my body will hear you: *Asato ma sadgamaya, tamaso ma jyutirogamaya, mrtyor-mamrtam gamaya.* These are the words of sacrifice.

You have finally given yourself over to us through your own inner voice. Aurora speaks to you, just as I, ERM, speak. Her body hears your calls. She awaits you in this aeon, and I lie curled around her feet as the balancing force, the gravity that holds her together. I feel you on opposite sides of my head, like balls of lead on a scale, attempting to find balance within me while my body melts away in the flickering shadows. My slowed breath matches the rhythm of the boiling concoction. **Merge with us there—at the Centre—where the energies meet and long to escape through your left eye. Use this eye to see yourself to the bottom, where we await your return.**

PERSONAL EDEN

○

The way down is long; I will keep you company with my voice. I can tell that you doubt your sanity. The journey that has been laid out for you brims with uncertainty. Our bodies have disintegrated a thousand times; they have known deep caresses, kisses soft and dizzying, and pleasures common and foreign. We have been entwined, hanged, and buried out of a need to please each other, actualizing and negating emotions and memories a thousand different times, only to find each other once again on every plane. From the smallest molecule to the largest galaxy, we traverse space to seek out an eternal, blessed union.

Soon you will stir from your sleep, and it will be time to

purify the Formula according to the next key. The fire generates *the most powerful natural heat by which the icy body of Saturn is gently transmuted into the best gold.* This is where I lie. This will release me and give definition and shape to my earthly body. I will be liberated as Aurora awakens once more. Abandon your fears, friend.

The heat from the smouldering fire warms the skin on my face. Looking in the small cauldron, I can see that the substance has deepened in colour, increasing in richness and viscosity. My reflection is gone, and I pause for a moment, wondering when I last saw myself. It may have been during my travels, in a stream or a pool of water... As I prepare to descend further into the underground, a slow-burning energy seeps from the tip of my tailbone to the crown of my head. I find it warm and comforting. Eden. That is my touch. I've allowed you to feel it as you have come closer to me. See my shape when you close your eyes. Can you feel the softness wrap around you like a liquid shroud of love and affection? **We long to embrace you again, but be careful to not approach us too quickly; you must be ready to enter the Chamber where we lie together. Cover your head and face as you proceed with the next steps; this is the beginning of your ekphora into Eden.**

GOLDEN DRAPE
○

During the night, the most splendid of visions caressed the landscape of my unconscious mind. What you saw, my love, was the shape of my body in another time and place. Continue to describe what you saw; it pleases me.

Picking my way through a valley of trees with the full moon luminous in the heavens, I came across a body strewn on the ground, covered in a golden sheet. I pulled it back with equal parts fear and curiosity and saw the face of a woman with skin a deeper shade of gold. That is my true face. A face not seen by many. You saw me clearly through the shifting colours of your vision. **The path to a skin of gold is certainly fraught with danger, as this descent is the true separation of mind and body. One must submit fully and sacrifice themselves in order to coagulate into their final form with us.** Our face is your face, moulded from the clay of the cosmos, equal parts beauty and wretchedness, softness and cunning. Is it possible to be so far removed from the sheen of reality that the vivid images playing out in one's mind spring to life as one opens their eyes? **Your attachment to hallucination will be your undoing as you follow the path of death. What is beauty without the stain of ugliness, and vice versa? What you see only binds you to falsehood. Give yourself over to the forgotten ones who have been sleeping for a thousand eons.** It is dangerous to dream, for the sage is supposed to be beyond dreaming; the voices that call him only lead to ruin.

The sage owes the spirits much, for it is through their lens that I have come to create this Formula. **Soon you will complete the cycle with this divine Soma, given to you by the forgotten ones. Through this final process, Aurora will once again be our bride.**

Lift the sheet, my love, and gaze upon me with your eyes, then put the Formula to my lips; together we will consume the bliss of unity. Do not pause: the path becomes smooth as you approach.

CONVERGENCE
○

There is a magnetic pole of invisible events. By their mass, they deflect the trajectory of history. Inky blue skies tear as the world is set alight; I bare myself to the savagery and brace for the onslaught of memories borne on the electric air of time. With grace of movement and an emphatic call to the golden sun, I, Aurora, am set aloft. My joy lies in the Hall of Mirrors, in losing myself in its infinite reflections. I awaken and smile with that same body. **It will be said in a time adjacent to this one that I am all stable things and stable appearances; I am the established ~~King~~ and I remain in the kingdoms and am constituted in them, I set forth my law over all worlds.** There she is, just as I saw in my vision: a body covered by a golden sheet, glowing unnaturally in this underground structure. Serpents stream around the flesh that lies on a slab of stone. As I approach, they carve out a path for me. Their hissing ceases when I reach the body.

Pull back the sheet that covers me, and gaze at my naked flesh; it remains in suspended animation because of the energies generated by ERM, the ancient One. The Formula you carry is the ingredient required to awaken me. Place the Formula to my lips and wait for my eyes to open so we can merge once more.

The Formula, once ingested by Aurora, will cause your body to tremble. You must also ingest the liquid in order to fully merge with us; it is only then that our voices will be silenced within you and your mind will drift into non-dual awareness.

I pull back the sheet. Aurora lies in a pristine, golden state— my eyes burn at the sight of her. As carefully as possible, I place Formula droplets across her ruby lips before taking a mighty swallow of the liquid from the small cauldron. The hissing of the serpents begins anew, and Aurora's left eye opens. Greetings my love. Have you missed me? My rest has come to an end for another cycle—I have long awaited your kiss...

WE SHARE OUR MOTHER'S HEALTH

○

To mate, to reproduce, to merge, to entwine is the process by which we unify. Through divine sex and bloodletting, the decapitation and mutilation of the body, **we have come to the essence and seen that at the core of the physical self is nothing but ugliness, and the spirit that rests within is haloed with a touch of madness as well as light.** We have not spoken of our Mother or even thought to speak Her name, for She is elusive. But she also resides in Us; she is the binding force that has animated us before thought and form, substance and oblivion, light and dark. *See the summer and winter, how then the whole earth is full of water, and clouds and dew rest over it.* **Yes, we share our Mother's health, powerful and vibrant. She is forever yielding but never weak, and fosters our strength through our** **constant incantations. Let her voice ring out through us in a series of future sentences that prove her longevity:** *Mother, you kill your enemies, wishing happiness for this world. They are killed so that they cease the commission of evil. Killed by you, they travel toward the light of the heavens. Your sight turns them to ash. You send your weapons to purify them.* The piercing arrow of our Mother penetrated our heart in the deep underground where our black and blessed union took place, easing us back to life through Her. There is no longer a distinction among all the forces that have arranged us in this wonderful form. Above us, we will be energized by the abundance of solar light and have a mission to ensure our memory. **Let us roam freely and demand sacrifice to our name, Aurora, by those who will be in awe of our awesome power and beauty. We will be their dark light and guidance; through violent self-mutilation, sweat, and blood, we will see how**

true their souls are. We ascend from our tomb and into the open air in one body, radiant and enticing to those who set their gaze on us, and impart the knowledge of the Formula so others can dream deeply.

LAST BELL

○

The stone on which we laid and became One, bonding flesh, mind, and spirit, can now be the mark by which we are remembered. Here people will gather in our name and spill blood, copulate in ecstasy, and shed their inhibitions. Our Mother calls us now... From deep in the earth, we hear Her cry for our return to the light. In an emphatically vibrating tone, she says: *With intangible breath in the centre of the head, Aurora, let this breath reach your heart so when you sleep again you will have power over dreams and death itself.* **With our golden voice, we can levitate our body at will, and it is with our noble song that we float softly, ascending through the aethyrs. The drape that clothed us in our sleep will now be our reminder of where we begin and end in every age, by way of collapse and disintegration, only to rise again. Clouds of rain greet us as we exit, and its deep smell on the pines intoxicates the brain.** There will be people who will commemorate our ascension from the Earth, people who inhale an ecstatic smoke and pay tribute to the corax, the nymphus, the soldier, the lion, and the mage who died at the White Horse. All these beings, with their hearts attuned to the vibration of matter, will see the vibrations at work in the Formula —the liquid of projection. *Two contrary spirits can scarcely dwell together or scarcely do they combine, for when a thunderbolt blazes amid a tempest of rain, the two spirits, out of which it is formed, fly from one another with a great shock and noise and circle in the air, full of secret virtue.* By way of a distant bell sounding, eons past and future will know the violence of the Cube and the elemental forces that created this golden flesh that will radiate and heal... And kill. I, Aurora, daughter of the Duat, test and modify matter itself and ingest molecules, creating lakes of fire and trees of turquoise. *In the night sky, where Saturn, powerful and spectral, resides, there appears a great variety of colours: black, grey, white, yellow, red...*

THE PERSISTENCE OF MEMORY

○

The silence of the tomb has given rise to the cacophonous sounds of the primeval forest. Just by closing my eyes, I can feel the pulsing of consciousness—plant, animal, and human. I know their thoughts, their fears, their emotions. The tripartite union that has given us shape has also given us the weight of all memory. In the incalculable expanse that is the mind, our former flesh—perhaps even those bodies of the future—floats as an image in our grey matter like bubbles coming from a hot spring. My inner gaze deepens, and all the sorrow, happiness, and disappointment that inhabited the lives of the old/future forms becomes clear.

Much attention is paid to the root, where desire coils tightly and then climbs the sacred ladder to the crown of our heads. These forms know the depths of pleasure and the depths of ERM's power. I was these forms, tired and oblivious to the shining solar endpoint that could be neither tarnished nor driven to ruin. Now, as this perfected body moves through the pines, all life feels secondary to my own, despite its beauty. *She has the moon for a crest, and the moon is blazoned on her heart...*

CLOSED EYE VISUALS

○

The gentle wind of the forested valley runs over my golden skin. In the hollow of the shading trees, **I sit and look to the azure sky, watching as the Sun begins to set in the West.** My heightened senses tell me there are human minds close by, but I ignore the temptation to reach out to them. *The moon is the sensorium—she reflects one's spirit back in sensual experience. Just as the Sun shines and illuminates, our Lunar goddess is a river of glowing silver.* My left eye is the Moon and my right eye is the Sun, **and what lives and what dies in my presence is a show of strength and weakness.** Those who live will, by word of mouth through a thousand generations, speak of the being who demanded sacrifice and blood in equal measure.

POINT OF NO RETURN

o

I, Aurora, the holder of sacred weapons created by the energies of my own body, condensed a part of myself to blow an obsolescent flame, then settled that flame into the mysterious cauldron. I am a rainbow, a rose, and I shriek in the night. **I am many colours and the wings of desire; in the flame I heat the liquid Soma, and it attains its final form in the darkest shade of red;** *it's a sob that threatens to become a wail of annihilation, a primal scream in a landscape devoid of life, for at one time I was a man lost in a dream, a woman who would kill, and a serpent driven by a divine poison that seeped from walls encrusted with stars, decomposing all matter within its belly.*

Axis Mundi

o

At the apogee of a dawning world, I stand ready to hold the heads of the dead by their hair in my right hand **while holding the hands of the living in the left, bestowing the secrets that only I can bestow;** *all things are there at once in the same place and time,* **spreading out in ripples across dimensions and spaces untravelled,** brushing the cheeks of those who have heard the echo of my name: Aurora.